GW00725965

Who's On First?

A NIGHTMARE COMEDY

by Jack Sharkey

SAMUEL FRENCH, INC.
45 West 25th Street NEW YORK, N.Y. 10010
7623 Sunset Boulevard HOLLYWOOD 90046
LONDON *TORONTO*

Printed in U.S.A.

ISBN 0 573 61812 7

STORY OF THE PLAY

Camille is giving a party. Don shows up in a jealous funk about his wife Alice, whom he suspects of seeing another man. When Alice and Ben have arrived, it turns out their relationship is innocent, but by then Don has accidentally shot Ben, Alice and even Camille. Camille, not realizing that an antique lamp she's bought just that day has supernatural powers, wishes that things might have turned out differently—and that is precisely what happens, as all concerned find themselves back at the party's beginning again—and again—and again—doomed to live the same hour over and over again until they get it right, thanks to the magical accident. Or *is* it an accident? Is it possible their dilemma is all part of someone's fiendish plan? Hold onto your hat—and your sides—as you wend your way through a labyrinth of hilarity to a real shocker of a surprise ending.

"WHO'S ON FIRST?" had its world premiere on September 17, 1975 at the Country Club Comedy Theatre, Mount Prospect, Illinois, under the direction of Tom Ventriss, with the following cast:

DON (The Husband?) .... *Kent Hageman*
CAMILLE (The Friend?) .... *Maggie Schmidt*
BEN (The Lover?) .... *Michael Jon Sims*
ALICE (The Wife?) .... *Cindy Flodin*

Setting and Lighting—*Larry Peterson*

Sound—*Tom Gaines*

Costumes and Props—*Bob Andrews*

Locale: Somebody's apartment, someplace

Time: The extreme present

ACT ONE

SCENE 1: A Friday evening, about 8 o'clock
SCENE 2: Same place, same time
SCENE 3: Exactly the same

ACT TWO

SCENE 1: As above
SCENE 2: Ditto
SCENE 3: What else?
SCENE 4: You guessed it!

ACT THREE

One more time . . .

Who's On First?

ACT ONE

SCENE 1

Curtain rises on the living room of a cozy apartment. Upstage Center is a large wardrobe, usable as a coat closet. Left of the wardrobe is the front door to the hallway of the apartment building; Right of the wardrobe is an entrance to a short corridor leading to the bedroom, bathroom and kitchen. Directly Center Stage is a low round cocktail table; near it, and angled toward it from above, Right and Left, are two low armchairs. Upstage Left, below the front door, is a small telephone table, bearing a phone and a phone book. A window is just below this, facing Left. Downstage Left is a small taboret, suitable for displaying objets d'art, *though its top is presently bare. Upstage Right, below corridor entrance, is a bar-cabinet, with plenty of bottles and glasses on top and on its shelves. Downstage Left is a long, low table holding record albums and a radio-phonograph. It is just going on 8 P.M., and lighting is cheery and bright.*

At curtain-rise, Stage is empty. Westminster-chime clock strikes eight. After a moment, CAMILLE *enters from corridor. She is young, pretty, and dressed for a party. She carries an ice bucket and an object wrapped in tissue paper. She sets the ice bucket on the bar, steps down to make a minute adjustment of one armchair, surveys the room like any anxious hostess hoping everything looks its best, then she moves down to taboret, unwrapping tissue-papered object. It proves to be a shiny oriental brass lamp, the sort that resembles a gravy-boat with a lid. She sets it on the taboret, steps back to study it, adjusts it a bit, seems satisfied, then starts toward corridor, balling up tissue paper with finality. As she reaches corridor entrance, DOORBELL rings. She stops, starts for door, stops again to look at balled-up tissue in her hand, hesitates, then turns and flings it off through corridor entrance, dusts off her palms against one another, and opens front door.* DON *enters. He wears a hat with low-pulled brim, a topcoat, collar turned up, and has his hands in topcoat pockets. We cannot see much of him, but when we can, he will prove to be a young man in his mid-twenties, not unpleasing of aspect. At the moment, however, his manner is quite distraught, and his voice is choked and near tears, and his words are slurred thanks to not-a-few earlier drinks, though he is not reeling-drunk, just fuddled.*

CAMILLE. Don!

DON. Camille—is Alice here?

CAMILLE. Alice? No—not yet, anyhow. I thought she'd be coming with *you* . . .

DON. Ha! (*Moves to bar as she closes door, pours himself a shot.*)

CAMILLE. (*Moving to him, concerned.*) Don, what is it? You seem upset . . .

DON. (*Tosses off drink, pours another during.*) Don't be ridiculous! Why should I be upset? These things happen all the time. Who am *I* to raise a fuss about it! (*Tosses off second drink, starts pouring another.*)

CAMILLE. What things? Don, are you feeling all right? (*Will follow him as he takes new drink down to Right armchair and sags into it, his face slack with despair.*) Is there anything I can do?

DON. Such as?

CAMILLE. Uh . . . Can I take your hat and coat?

DON. No. (*Swallows about half his drink.*)

CAMILLE. You're going to sit there like that all evening?

DON. Of course not. Just till Alice gets here. (*Ominously.*) And *then—!*

CAMILLE. (*Fearfully.*) And *then—?*

DON. *You'll* see! (*Tosses off remainder of drink.*) *Boy*, will you see!

CAMILLE. (*Takes shotglass, hesitates, then says, hostess-like but uncertainly.*) Would you—like another?

DON. Probably not. I didn't like the three I just had.

CAMILLE. (*Taking glass back to bar.*) Then why—?

DON. I'm getting my courage up. There's something I've got to do. Something I should have done before now!

CAMILLE. (*Setting glass on bar, offers hopefully.*) You're going to take off your hat and coat?

DON. Ha! (*Uncoils from armchair almost in a leap to his feet.*) If you knew—if you only knew—! (*Abruptly buries his face in his hands.*) Ah, the hell with it!

CAMILLE. (*Comes back down to him.*) Come on, Don —relax. This is supposed to be a party. (*Places a sympathetic hand on his shoulder.*) Here, let me take your coat— (*Recoils as he uncovers his face and pulls away.*) I'm sorry, I didn't mean to—

DON. No-no, *I'm* sorry. And *you* didn't do anything! Don't pay any attention to me. It's just— Oh, damn, I've got to get out of here! (*Starts Upstage toward front door.*) Make my excuses to the other guests, will you?

CAMILLE. (*Following him.*) But—Don—what *are* your excuses? What's the matter? Why are you behaving this way?

DON. (*Stops, turns, takes her hands.*) Camille—dear Camille—you're such a good friend. I only wish—

CAMILLE. What, Don? What do you wish—?

DON. (*Takes breath, then suddenly drops her hands.*) I wish I had another drink.

CAMILLE. (*Glad to do anything to cheer him.*) Here, I'll get it! (*Hurries to bar, as he just stands there.*) Would you like a little soda with it this time? Some ice?

DON. No. The straight stuff is just fine . . . (*As she pours, back to him, he takes a huge revolver out of his coat pocket, stares at it mournfully, then drops hand holding it to his side and sighs; she turns, coming back to him with drink; he suddenly raises it toward her.*) Do you see *this?!* (CAMILLE'S *eyes bug out, and both hands go up over her head, the drink flying out of the glass.*)

CAMILLE. Yes! Yes, I see it! Very pretty! Now put it away!

DON. Oh, for heaven's sake, put your hands down! This isn't for you!

CAMILLE. (*Hands still raised like a stickup victim's.*) I wouldn't take it if it was! I hate guns!

DON. Oh, okay, okay! (*Jams gun back into pocket.*) There, do you feel better now?

CAMILLE. (*Drops hands, lurches toward bar.*) Not quite . . . (*Pours shot into glass she holds, then drains it.*) *Now* I feel a little better. . . .

DON. I'm sorry if I scared you.

CAMILLE. That's all right. I think prematurely gray hair is becoming. (*Fingers go to her hair.*) Does it show yet?

DON. Aw, Camille. Poor Camille. I'm spoiling your party.

CAMILLE. What party? . . . *Oh!* I always forget things when my mind goes blank with fear.

DON. (*Starts for door again.*) I'd better get out of here!

CAMILLE. (*Runs to him, takes his arm.*) But you can't! Not like this! Sit down, relax, tell·me all about it.

DON. I don't want to sit down, and I can't relax, and—and—well, maybe I *will* tell you all about it!

CAMILLE. Good. And I'll make us *both* a drink! (*As she puts ice cubes and whisky into two tumblers, he comes tragically Down Left, stopping before taboret, but not looking down at it, staring out front unhappily, and speaks without looking back toward her.*)

DON. It's all such a terrible nightmare. A week ago, I would have laughed if you'd said such a thing could happen to *me* . . .

CAMILLE. I was out of town a week ago.

DON. That's a shame. I could have used the laugh.

CAMILLE. But Don, what *did* happen to you—? (*Will complete drink-fixing and join him.*) You've always been so upbeat and jolly . . .

DON. (*Turns head toward her as she approaches.*) Really? I always thought I was kind of a drag.

CAMILLE. (*Handing him drink.*) Nonsense. Why your face is full of laugh-lines. (*Touches outside corner of each eye with her finger, on:*) Here and here.

DON. Those aren't laugh-lines. I squint a lot.

CAMILLE. Come on, now. Be serious. What's troubling you, Don?

DON. (*Facing out front as before.*) Alice has a lover. (CAMILLE *reacts, but his head has hung down in shame, and he sees lamp on table, and points to it in interest.*) Hey, what's this?

CAMILLE. (*Not to be sidetracked.*) A lamp. What did you say about Alice and a lover—?

DON. (*Picking up lamp, quite sidetracked.*) She's seeing another guy. You know, this is very interesting.

CAMILLE. I'm sure it is. What other guy?

DON. I don't know his name. Gee, this metal is so shiny . . .

CAMILLE. It's only brass. Tell me about this other guy.

DON. I don't know a thing about him. This lamp reminds me of something . . .

CAMILLE. Aladdin. But you must know *something* about him, Don—!?

DON. Only that Alice has been seeing him. You mean if I rub this (*Rubs to demonstrate.*) I'll get my wish? (*Faint WIND noise as he rubs, but it ceases on:*)

CAMILLE. For all I know. *When* has Alice been seeing him, *where?!*

DON. I saw them both together on Wednesday at the Rexall soda fountain, having tuna salad sandwiches. (*Sets lamp down on taboret.*)

CAMILLE. Don, there's nothing sinister about tuna salad!

DON. I know; it was what she *answered* when I *asked* her. How much did you pay for this thing?

CAMILLE. Five dollars. When you asked her *what?*

DON. What she'd been doing on Wednesday. Hey, you got a bargain.

CAMILLE. I'm not so sure about that! You mean Alice didn't mention having lunch with this guy?

DON. She didn't even mention having lunch! Then why did you buy it?

CAMILLE. For a conversation piece, and it's working much too well! (*Takes his arm, tows him Upstage toward armchairs.*) Here, now, you sit down and tell me everything. There must be a perfectly good reason why Alice had tuna salad with a strange man at the Rexall soda fountain.

DON. (*Stopping before Left armchair but not sitting.*) That's what I told myself.

CAMILLE. So—?

DON. So why didn't she *tell* me she had tuna salad

with another man when I asked her what she was doing on Wednesday?

CAMILLE. Maybe it wasn't worth mentioning.

DON. Ha!

CAMILLE. Don, use your head. Would *you* tell your wife you were two-timing her over *tuna salad?* (*As he reacts, corrects herself.*) I mean, she's *not* two-timing you, Don! But who the hell remembers lunch at Rexall's?!

DON. But I asked her! I said, "Where did you have lunch?" And you know what she said? She said she didn't remember!

CAMILLE. See? That proves my point! Nobody remembers tuna salad! Do *you?*

DON. Don't try to protect her!

CAMILLE. Answer my question! Do you remember every time you have tuna salad?

DON. Of course I do! It gives me a rash.

CAMILLE. Oh, for—! Don, you're making something out of nothing!

DON. *Nothing?!* And just what do you consider *this—?!* (*On final word, reaches into coat pocket opposite that in which the revolver is stashed, and whips out a rubber chicken.*) Is *that* nothing?! (*Mournfully takes large swallow of drink.*)

CAMILLE. (*Stares at chicken till he finishes drinking; then.*) That's a rubber chicken!?

DON. I know. (*Means the situation.*) Isn't is horrible?

CAMILLE. (*Means the chicken.*) Well—it *would* take some getting *used* to—! (*Takes large swallow of drink as he slowly reacts to her lack of comprehension of his meaning.*)

DON. I don't mean the *chicken!* I mean *about* the chicken!

CAMILLE. *What* about the chicken?

DON. I found it when I searched our apartment. It was hidden. At the bottom of her underwear drawer.

(*Chokes on a sob on last line, takes another large swallow.*) *Now* do you blame me?

CAMILLE. Well, I certainly can't blame *Alice!*

DON. For having this rubber chicken?

CAMILLE. For *hiding* it! I mean—just *look* at it! All dangly and scrawny, no feathers—

DON. But don't you know what this *means—?!*

CAMILLE. What? What *could* it mean?

DON. (*A wrenching sob of misery.*) I don't *know!* That's what's *killing* me! (*Sags down into armchair, tosses off rest of his drink.*)

CAMILLE. Don—why were you searching the apartment in the first place?

DON. To find something—anything—that would prove to me, one way or the other, about Alice and this other man—! A photograph, a letter, a diary—! Instead, I found . . . *this!*

CAMILLE. (*As he sorrowfully stuffs chicken back into his pocket.*) It must have been a terrible shock.

DON. (*Shuddering at the memory, and nodding.*) I thought it was a snake with a big belly.

CAMILLE. Even so, Don—it may be a little *strange*—okay, a *lot* strange—but there's certainly nothing *incriminating* about it—!

DON. (*Hands her his empty glass.*) That's what I like about you, Camille. You always stick up for people.

CAMILLE. Look. Don. When she gets here tonight—why don't you just *ask* her, outright? Tell her what you know, and then say, "How come?"!

DON. (*Flings his arms up high, then slaps palms onto his knees for emphasis, standing up at the same moment.*) But what *do* I know?! What do you say to a wife who eats tuna salad behind your back and hides rubber chickens in her underwear drawer? (*Gives an example.*) "Who is this man you've been secretly seeing, and don't try to lie to me, because I found your chicken!" (*Moans.*) I not only can't figure it out, I can't even formulate a sensible question!

CAMILLE. (*Seeing the sense in this, suggests:*) Maybe you shouldn't try to solve both mysteries at once. (*Finishes her own drink, starts for bar with glasses.*) Take it in easy stages. First of all, ask her about that rendezvous at Rexall's, Don. I mean, you've *got* to give Alice a chance to *explain!* (*Sets glasses on bar.*)

DON. Explain? Could *you* explain?

CAMILLE. Well—*no*—but, I'm not *guilty* of anything— (*Cringes slightly as he advances toward her.*)

DON. Aha! Then you *do* think she's guilty!

CAMILLE. Of course not! I'm sure there's a very simple explanation! . . . I just can't think of one.

DON. Me neither! That's what hurts—not knowing! It's driving me mad! (*Clutches her by the shoulders, on:*) *Mad,* do you hear me? *Mad!*

CAMILLE. Oh, Don! Don't get mad!

DON. (*Releases her, spins away, heels of hands at his temples.*) I've got to get out of here! Take a long walk in the fresh air! (*Is moving toward front door.*) Think! Before I do something desperate!

CAMILLE. (*Following after him.*) Don! No! Wait! You can't go *out* of here this way!

DON. (*Reverses movement.*) All right, I'll go out the back way!

CAMILLE. (*Palms upon his chest.*) I mean in your condition!

DON. I'm as sober as you are!

CAMILLE. That's not saying much. (*PHONE rings.*) Oh, damn! Now look, stay right here, and don't go away! (*Hurries to answer phone.*)

DON. (*Stands distraught as she picks up phone.*) But there's no telling *what* I might do—!

CAMILLE. (*Waves at him to be silent, then speaks on phone, her back to him.*) Hello? . . . *Alice!* (*Pleasantly.*) We were just talking about you! . . . Me and Don . . . Yes, he's here . . . (*Out of her view,* DON *shuffles disconsolately toward front door; during her conversation, he will grasp knob, then stop and consider, then very slyly move back to wardrobe, make sure that she is not looking his way, and then get inside wardrobe and close the door.*) What? . . . Oh, really, who? . . . But *why* can't you tell me? . . . What *kind* of surprise? . . . Well, no, I don't *mind*, but . . . All right, but hurry! (*Hangs up, speaks toward where* DON *was as she turns.*) Alice has asked a friend along, but she won't tell me who he— Don? (*Looks around, peeks out front door, recloses it, stands uncertainly, then goes to bar and picks up what's left of her drink, muses a moment, then shrugs, drains drink, sets it down; DOORBELL rings; her eyes widen hopefully.*) Oh, good, he came back! (*Rushes to door, pulls it open on:*) Don—!? Oh, I'm sorry, I thought— (*Steps back as* BEN *enters; he is a handsome young man, very dapper in a tuxedo, and flamboyant of manner.*)

BEN. Hi, I'm Ben. And you must be— (*Puts fingers to temples like a stage mentalist, then points at her as if deducing.*) Camille!

CAMILLE. Ben?

BEN. Didn't Alice phone and tell you—?

CAMILLE. Oh, *you're* the one! (*Satisfied, closes front door.*)

BEN. The one?

CAMILLE. Well, you know how women who live alone feel about letting strange men into their apartments.

BEN. No, *how* do they feel about it?

CAMILLE. (*Meaning "Isn't the answer* obvious?!") Well, you're *in*, aren't you?! (*Laughs giddily, starts for bar.*) Can I fix you a drink?

BEN. (*Sizing up room, striding about very stagily, as if performing at all times for an audience.*) Oh, sure. Thanks. This is certainly a nice place you have here.

CAMILLE. (*Splashing whisky over ice.*) I never know

what to say when people tell me that. I mean, why would I live here if it *wasn't* a nice place, so I feel dumb if I say, "Oh, do you really think so?" but I feel even dumber if I say, "It sure is!" (*Comes to him with drink, he takes it.*)

BEN. Thanks. Aren't you having one?

CAMILLE. I don't know if I should. I just had one. (*Tries to get a reaction.*) With *Don—!*

BEN. (*Looks around.*) Don?

CAMILLE. Alice *did* tell you about *Don,* didn't she?

BEN. Huh? Oh, sure she did. I was just wondering where he was.

CAMILLE. He left.

BEN. So soon? I was looking forward to meeting him.

CAMILLE. You were?

BEN. Shouldn't I be?

CAMILLE. Well, it's just— I mean—oh—*you* know . . .

BEN. No.

CAMILLE. Well, maybe he'll be back. He just wanted to take a walk—I think . . . (*DOORBELL.*) Oh, maybe that's Don now! (*Heads toward door.*) I know he'll be anxious to meet *you,* and— (*Has pointed finger in cocked-gun position on "you" and now reacts to her own gesture, remembering gun, and stops short of door.*) Listen. Ben. Would you mind awfully doing me a favor?

BEN. Oh, sure. What?

CAMILLE. (*Points down corridor.*) There's some tissue paper there in the hall. Would you take it into the kitchen and toss it in the garbage?

BEN. (*At sea, but amiable, sets drink on bar.*) Uh, why—sure thing! (*Exits into corridor.*)

CAMILLE. (*Looks anxiously after him for a moment, then pulls open door, reacts with surprise as* ALICE*—a lovely young woman in a beautiful party dress—sails airily in.*) Alice! It's you!

ALICE. Of course it's me. Who else were you expecting? (*As* CAMILLE *peeks out through door, then leans back inside and closes it:*) Or hasn't Ben shown up yet?

CAMILLE. Actually, I thought it might be Don.

ALICE. Don? Isn't he here? On the phone, you said—

CAMILLE. He went out. But he may be back at any time, and I think there's something you should know—! (*Stops as* BEN *comes back into room.*)

ALICE. Ben! You *did* get here! I'm *so* glad! (*Takes his hand.*)

CAMILLE. Listen, kids, I want to tell you something—

BEN. (*To* ALICE.) It was easy. You give very good directions. (*Takes drink from bar.*)

ALICE. Well, I certainly wouldn't want *you* to miss the party! Not with the big surprise we have for Don!

CAMILLE. Please, I've got to tell you about—! . . . *What* surprise for Don?

BEN. Well, it's sort of a secret . . .

ALICE. Don doesn't know anything about it!

CAMILLE. I wouldn't be too *sure* about that—!

ALICE. But what could he possibly know? We've been so careful!

CAMILLE. Not quite careful enough.

BEN. There, I *knew* it wouldn't work! (*Takes quick sip from drink, sets glass on bar.*) Alice, we should never have started this—!

ALICE. Oh, Ben, don't be so nervous! Camille, how *much* does Don know?

CAMILLE. Not an *awful* lot . . . I mean, he knows there's *something* going on, but he's not sure *what.*

ALICE. Oh, good, then we have nothing to worry about!

CAMILLE. Well, I wouldn't say *that,* either—! I've never seen him so upset.

BEN. Upset? Now I *am* getting nervous! Alice, we should never have tried to fool him!

ALICE. Perhaps you're right—but—it seemed such a *harmless* little deception—

CAMILLE. You wouldn't say that if you could have seen *Don!*

BEN. What do you mean?

ALICE. Yes, what did he do? What did he say?

CAMILLE. Does tuna salad sandwiches at Rexall's ring a bell—?

BEN. You mean—?

ALICE. Last Wednesday—?

CAMILLE. He was there. He saw everything!

ALICE. Oh, *no!* He *didn't!*

DON. (*Flings both wardrobe doors open and steps out, revolver pointed toward them, simultaneous with his line.*) *Oh* yes he did! (*Others react with horror, take a terrified backstep.*)

CAMILLE. Don!

BEN. Oh, no!

DON. Oh, yes!

ALICE. Wait, darling, I can explain—!

(*As* DON *takes another step forward,* BEN *backs to Right, just in front of bar,* ALICE *backs more toward Downstage Right, and* CAMILLE *backs almost directly Downstage toward armchairs.*)

DON. It's too late for explanations!

ALICE. Don, are you crazy? Put that gun down!

DON. Not until I'm through using it!

CAMILLE. Don, use your head, you can't just start shooting at people—!

DON. Stop where you are, all of you! I'm dead serious! (*They stop, each about five feet from him in their various directions, their hands going up almost by unthinking reflex-action, as* DON *hoists rubber chicken into view with his weaponless hand and waves it aloft.*) Perhaps *this* will show you just *how* serious!

ALICE. Don! You've been in my underwear!

BEN. (*Not sure how to take this.*) *Really—?!*

ALICE. I mean he's been going through my drawers!

BEN. (*Still taking it wrong, nods.*) That's what I *thought* you meant. . . !

CAMILLE. Don, will you put down that chicken, you're making me nervous!

DON. Alice, this is your last chance! I demand an explanation! Who *is* this man?! (*Jabs gun at* BEN *for emphasis.*)

BEN. (*Babbling with fear.*) Tell him! Tell him!

ALICE. Ben is a magician!

DON. (*Gun-hand sagging just a bit.*) A *what?*

ALICE. I was taking magic lessons!

CAMILLE. Oh, Alice, you can do better than *that!*

ALICE. But it's true! I was doing it for Don!

DON. For me? What are you talking about?

ALICE. (*All in one panicky breath.*) Well, the last time we went to a party, and Marge McNertny played the piano, and Sally Weemis gave poetry recitations, you said to me why didn't *I* get up and do something like those *other* wives, but I didn't know anything about music or poetry, so I decided to take lessons so maybe I could do some card tricks!

DON. *Card tricks?!*

ALICE. (*Semi-lowering hands.*) You wanta see one?

CAMILLE. (*Doing same, taking one step in direction of corridor.*) I'll get the cards—

DON. (*Brings up revolver.*) Hold it! (*Others back-step, hands going even higher.*) That still doesn't explain this rubber chicken!

ALICE. Of course it does!

CAMILLE. It does?

ALICE. I couldn't find a rubber rabbit!

DON. (*Wavering.*) Alicc—is this *true—?!*

BEN. (*Starts to reach inside left side of jacket with right hand.*) Let me show you my union card—

DON. (*Gestures at him with gun, which fires on final word of:*) Not so fast—! (BEN *gives yelp and clutches stomach,* DON *gets all flustered.*) Oo, gee, *I'm* sorry—!

ALICE. (*Palms to her temples, shrieks.*) You've *shot* him!

DON. (*Embarrassed and apologetic, turns face toward her, but gestures toward still-moaning* BEN *with gun, on:*) All I meant to do was—! (*Gun fires again,* BEN *gives new yelp, clutches abdomen with other hand.*) Oh, gosh, I did it again!

CAMILLE. (*Rushes up toward him.*) Don, will you stop *gesturing—?!*

DON. (*Faces her, makes vague gesture toward* BEN, *who is still ad-libbing gasping yelps, holding himself in two places, as* ALICE *starts forward to help him.*) I was only trying to emphasize my words by—! (*Gun fires again, at lower angle, and* ALICE *shrieks, shot in the foot, holding injured foot in both hands and hopping about on the other, yelping in counterpoint with* BEN.) Oh, golly—! (*Brings gun up before his face, staring at it stupidly.*) I should never have oiled the trigger—!

CAMILLE. (*Grabs gun by barrel, pulls it toward herself.*) Give me that thing, you idiot—!

DON. Camille, *stop,* my finger's caught in the trigger-thing—!

CAMILLE. (*Up tight against him, the revolver between them.*) If you'll just stop clenching your *hand—!* (*Gun fires; she stares at him, expressionless, for one moment, then her mouth opens in a gape of shock.*) Oh boy! Wow! *Now* you've done it! (*Lurches Downstage Left, one hand clutching her side at waist.*) Ow, does that smart—!

DON. (*Starting to sob.*) Oh! Oh! Oh! What am I doing?! What have I done?!

(BEN *has by now lurched and stumbled down to armchairs, and fallen back into Right armchair, still yelping piteously, holding stomach and abdomen, his eyes wide and glassy with shock, while* ALICE *continues her solo dance up near the bar, and* CAMILLE *moves slowly Downstage Left with faltering footsteps, clutching her side, and* DON *sits, sobbing and blubbering, on Right arm of Left armchair, taking handkerchief from* BEN'S *breast pocket to wipe his streaming eyes—except that, magician-fashion, in colorful array—the kerchief is knotted corner-to-corner with a long chain of bright silk kerchiefs or scarves which sag like a rainbow bridge between* BEN'S *breast and* DON'S *eyes, and keep emerging one by one as* DON *pulls one after the other to his eyes to wipe away the ceaseless tears, and as* ALICE *yelps,* BEN *moans, and* DON *sobs, a gasping* CAMILLE *sags, near taboret, her left hand going out for support onto the top of the brass lamp, her right hand still upon her wound, and:*)

CAMILLE. (*As if with her final breath:*) Oh, how I wish this whole thing had never happened! If only there were some way to go back—to straighten things out—to make everything come out right—! (*There comes an eerie whistle of WIND, and lights start to dim upon everything Onstage except* CAMILLE *and the brass lamp, which she looks down upon in wonder, and remarks:*) What the hell . . . ?!

HOLLOW DISEMBODIED VOICE. (*Over WIND.*) Go back . . . straighten things out . . . Go back . . . go back . . . go back . . . go back . . . (*WIND and* VOICE *fade into:*)

BLACKOUT

ACT ONE

SCENE 2

Still in the darkness of the blackout, we hear a Westminster-chime clock striking eight; darkness prevails during the sixteen-tone melody, and the first four strokes of the hour, but begins to lighten on the fifth stroke, and the Stage will be at full brightness by the stroke of eight. Setting is exactly the same as at the top of Scene One. After a moment, as before, CAMILLE *enters with ice bucket and tissue-wrapped package, goes through exactly the same business up till the DOORBELL rings. Then:*

CAMILLE. (*Still holding balled-up tissue, opens front door.*) Alice!

ALICE. (*Enters in same party dress as before.*) I hope I'm not too early—?

CAMILLE. (*Shuts door.*) Maybe just a smidgeon . . . (*Holds up tissue in explanation, starts off into corridor.*) Let me ditch this and I'll be right with you. Where's Don, parking the car?

ALICE. (*As* CAMILLE *exits.*) Actually, I don't know. I came by cab.

CAMILLE. (*Off.*) Oh, I *hope* you don't mean he's not *coming—?!*

ALICE. I don't know that, either. He's been acting funny lately. Tonight, after dinner, he said he wanted to take a walk, to think things over. . . .

CAMILLE. (*Re-entering minus tissue.*) What things?

ALICE. I don't know. He didn't explain, and I didn't exactly want to press him for details—you know how Don gets when you push him too hard!

CAMILLE. Who doesn't! Would you like a drink?

ALICE. No, I think I'll wait awhile.

CAMILLE. Well, then, shall we sit down—? (*Leads way to armchairs, where she will sit Left,* ALICE *Right.*) I've been on my feet all afternoon getting the place cleaned up for the party.

ALICE. It looks just lovely, Camille. . . . (*Notices brass lamp.*) Is that a new lamp?

CAMILLE. (*Nods.*) Just picked it up yesterday. An antique, I think.

ALICE. It's very nice. How do you plug it in?

CAMILLE. You don't. I think you either light it with a match or rub it till smoke comes out of the spout.

ALICE. That's nice.

CAMILLE. (*Suspiciously.*) Or stand on your head and spit at it.

ALICE. Oh.

CAMILLE. (*Sharply enough to snap* ALICE *out of her funk.*) You haven't heard a word I said!

ALICE. I'm sorry. It's Don. I'm so worried about him.

CAMILLE. And you came to the party without him?

ALICE. Well— I didn't know what *else* to do when he didn't come back. I mean, if I stayed there, he might come *here,* or—well—*you* know. So I got dressed, and left him a note saying I'd gone, and I came over alone.

CAMILLE. Aw, what a shame. I do hope he remembers to show up. *Sure* you wouldn't like that drink?

ALICE. Oh—maybe a small one.

CAMILLE. (*Rising and heading for bar.*) How *small?*

ALICE. Whatever *you're* having'll be fine. One size is as good as another. . . . (*As* CAMILLE *fixes a pair of drinks, she sighs; then:*) Do you *know* what's wrong with Don—? (*It is a preliminary, not a question, so* CAMILLE *only jests:*)

CAMILLE. I think so, but I've misplaced my list. (*Continues fixing drinks.*)

ALICE. I'm serious.

CAMILLE. I know, sweetie. I was only trying to cushion the moment. (*Will return to her chair with drinks for both of them during:*) Are you sure you really want to discuss *Don?* I mean, we're supposed to be here for a good time . . .

ALICE. (*Taking drink as* CAMILLE *sits.*) Oh, this is nothing *bad.* I'm not going to sob on your *shoulder* or anything. I'm just kind of figuring out loud. . . .

CAMILLE. Okay, then, if those are the ground-rules. *What's* wrong with Don?

ALICE. He *thinks!*

CAMILLE. Are you slurring your words *already?*

ALICE. No, really, I mean it. He never takes anything as a matter of course. He's always looking for hidden motives, deeper meanings to things that don't even have *shallow* meanings—!

CAMILLE. Such as what?

ALICE. Like. . . . Like if I'm ten minutes late coming home from shopping, he's all ready to call the police, because he's sure I've been kidnapped or cracked up the car or—or— Of course, actually, it's kind of *flattering,* this concern of his, and I'm *glad* he thinks about me when I'm not around, but—well—it really gets to be a drag, sometimes!

CAMILLE. I wish someone would worry about *me* like that! If *I* vanished from the face of the earth, nobody would get upset except my *landlord!* And not till the first of the month!

ALICE. But he worries about *other* things, too! Like am I finding fulfillment!

CAMILLE. Well, *are* you—?

ALICE. I don't really even *want* the kind of fulfillment *Don's* talking about! You remember Luella's party, last month, when Marge McNertny did the belly dance, and Sally Weemis recited all those dirty limericks—?

CAMILLE. (*Doesn't know why this memory puzzles her, sets drink on table and holds fingertips to temples a moment; then:*) I—I remember them doing *something* at the party, but—somehow— (*Shakes head, picks up drink and sips at it.*) Oh, never mind, I must be getting senile. Go ahead.

ALICE. Well, Don got worried that I felt left out. He kept insisting that *I* find something to do, so *I* could feel fulfilled!

CAMILLE. So what did you do?

ALICE. I met this man—

CAMILLE. (*Reacts.*) Now, hold on, I don't think Don wants you to get *that* fulfilled—!

ALICE. Oh, dear, I almost forgot! I asked him to come to your *party* tonight!

CAMILLE. (*Starts to rise.*) That's just great! Excuse me while I go hide all the sharp knives—!

ALICE. Camille, don't be silly, it's not what you think!

CAMILLE. You're right. It's not what *I* think. It's what *Don's* going to think! (*Starts for kitchen.*)

ALICE. (*Rises and stops her.*) Camille, will you *listen?!* This man means *nothing* to me. I only *hired* him for a little while to *teach* me a few things—!

CAMILLE. *Oh,* your husband is just going to be *crazy* about *that!* (*DOORBELL.*)

ALICE. That must be him now!

CAMILLE. The one who teaches, or the one who thinks?

ALICE. What's the difference?!

CAMILLE. (*Hesitates, fingertips to temples again.*) I—I don't *know*—but—it's the strangest thing—there's something about that threshold there. . . .

ALICE. Camille, do you feel all right?

CAMILLE. I guess so—but it just seems that it will make a big difference—when I open that door—who's on that threshold *right now*—

ALICE. What *possible* difference could it make if Ben's on the threshold first, or Don's on the threshold first, or even *who's* on first—?

CAMILLE. (*Gives shake of head, recovers composure.*) You're right. I'm being stupid. (*DOOR-

BELL.) Coming—! (*Opens door;* BEN *enters, dressed as before, same stagy entrance.*)

BEN. Hi, I'm Ben. And you must be— (*Same business.*) Camille! (*Stares at her as she blinks and touches herself on forehead.*) What's the matter?

CAMILLE. (*Shivers, recovers.*) Oooh! Sorry. (*As she ushers him in and closes door:*) Did you ever have one of those things—one of those creepy moments when you say to yourself, "I've been here *before*— I've *done* this before—*said* this before—!"?

ALICE. Don't be silly, Camille. You've never met Ben.

CAMILLE. No—that's for sure. I haven't. But for just a moment then— Oh, the hell with it! Hi, Ben! (*Clasps his hand.*) Make yourself at home. Can I fix you a drink?

BEN. Oh, sure, anything at all. Hi, Alice. Nice of you to invite me to your friend's party.

ALICE. Oh, it's a pleasure. So glad you could make it.

CAMILLE. (*Fixing a drink for* BEN.) Yeah, don't mind *me!* I only *live* here!

BEN. Hey, listen, if I'm in the *way* or anything—?!

CAMILLE. No-no, really. There's loads to eat and drink. As a matter of fact, I *like* surprises. The only problem is— (*Comes to* BEN *with drink.*) there are certain *other* people who might not be quite as accomodating.

BEN. (*Grasps her meaning, says accusingly to* ALICE:) You *haven't* told *Don. Have* you!

ALICE. I—I was waiting for the right moment. . . .

CAMILLE. (*With an upsurge of zest.*) Listen, this gala event is going down in quicksand! (*Heads for radio-phonograph.*) Let's have a little music and liven things up a bit! (*Will turn on radio during:*) When Alice's right moment comes along, I want the mood to be merry! (*A pleasant foxtrot plays softly on RADIO.*)

BEN. (*Takes* ALICE'S *drink, sets hers and his on cocktail table.*) Dance—?

ALICE. Love to! (*They dance till they are just Downstage Right of cocktail table, and* CAMILLE *is moving toward bar, when DOORBELL rings.*)

CAMILLE. Whoops! (*Reverses field, charges down and takes* BEN *from* ALICE.) May I cut in?! Alice, *you* get the door!

ALICE. But—? Oh! (*Gets the message, starts for door as* CAMILLE *and* BEN *dance, will open it to admit a somber* DON, *garbed as before.*) Darling! You *did* come! I was getting concerned. (*Takes his hat and coat, revealing him in a fairly presentable suit, and hangs his outer things in wardrobe, during:*)

CAMILLE. (*Waves without stopping the dance.*) Hi, Don! Grab a partner and join us!

BEN. Camille, can you waltz a little faster, this is a foxtrot! (CAMILLE *laughs, and they stop dancing as* DON *joins them, and MUSIC lowers, becoming barely audible.*)

DON. (*Not quite gloomy, but very subdued.*) Hi. Sorry I'm late. I took a walk. Had a lot on my mind. Forgot the time. (*Looks curiously at* BEN.)

CAMILLE. Oh! Don, I'd like you to meet Ben!

DON. (*As he shakes hands with* BEN, *looks at* CAMILLE *on:*) Ben what?

CAMILLE. Ben wh—? Oh! Uh . . . well . . . um . . . ?

ALICE. (*Has just come down to them from wardrobe.*) Oh, what's in a name!?

BEN. (*As* DON *reacts to her arrival, pumps his hand enthusiastically.*) I'm happy to meet you, Don! Alice has told me so much about you!

DON. Really? I thought you two had just met.

ALICE. Oh, we did!

CAMILLE. She talked real fast while I was out in the kitchen making hors d'oeuvres!

DON. (*Looks about vaguely.*) I don't see any hors d'oeuvres—?

CAMILLE. They looked so good I ate them myself!

DON. I knew I should have come early!

ALICE. That's all right, darling, I'll go make some more! (*Starts for kitchen.*)

BEN. I'll help you carry them in! (*Follows her toward kitchen.*)

CAMILLE. (*Sees* DON *scowling after them, tries to distract him.*) Don, why *didn't* you come earlier! I was surprised when Alice showed up— (*To stress non-hanky-panky:*) *alone.*

DON. (*Miserable, glad to confide in someone.*) I've been having problems—strange problems—so strange I'm not sure I could even explain them to a psychiatrist. . . !

CAMILLE. Oh, we all have our off-days—

DON. But this weird obsession doesn't stop! I keep finding things around the apartment—things I can't account for—and when I ask Alice about them, she says she knows nothing about them, either! That leaves me two choices—either Alice isn't telling me the truth, or I've been bringing the stuff in myself, and then forgetting about it! I don't know which is worse!

CAMILLE. I don't understand, Don. What kind of things?

DON. Things like— Well, let me show you something I found just this afternoon. (*Reaches into inner jacket pocket, produces first of a long string of rainbow-varied magician's-silks, hands it to her, keeps pulling out more and more of chain and piling silks up on her outstretched hands as he talks.*) Look at this! . . . And this and this! . . . Did you ever see anything so bewildering in your life? . . . What can they possibly *mean—?!*

CAMILLE. (*Speaks just as* BEN, *followed by* ALICE, *emerges from corridor, bearing a small platter of hors d'oeuvres;* CAMILLE, *naturally, thinks she is making a tension-relieving joke as she says:*) Search me! Maybe your wife has been having secret meetings with a magician! (*Starts laughing, sees* BEN'S *and* ALICE'S *stricken faces, gets the message, stops laughing, but then forces a smile as a suddenly credulous* DON *turns to stare at her.*)

DON. Do you know—that could be *it!*

CAMILLE. (*Now knowing it* is *it, says desperately, dropping kerchiefs onto table:*) Nonsense! I was joking! Why would Alice do a silly thing like that?!

ALICE. (*With sickly brightness, as if she hadn't heard.*) A silly thing like *what,* Camille—?

CAMILLE. Oh, look, they've brought the hors d'oeuvres!

BEN. (*Holding out platter with a flourish.*) *Presto!* (*As* DON *stares narrow-eyed at him and* ALICE *and* CAMILLE *wince.*) Uh . . . . that's the brand-name! "Presto Cheese and Crackers!" (*Puts platter down, to left of piled kerchiefs.*)

DON. These look like anchovies.

CAMILLE. Presto doesn't keep very well. (*Before* DON *can quite reach one to taste it, grabs him in her embrace.*) Let's dance! (*MUSIC comes up to normal volume.*)

BEN. Great idea! (*Starts dancing off with* ALICE.)

DON. (*Watching them with suspicion as* CAMILLE *twirls him desperately about the floor.*) I didn't know Alice could dance that well—!

CAMILLE. (*Before she can bite her tongue.*) Maybe she's been practicing! (Now *she bites her tongue.*)

ALICE. (*Sensing disaster.*) Hey, let's switch partners!

CAMILLE. Yes, let's! (*All release partner, moving in rhythm to music, and start dancing with new partner —then realize that* DON *is dancing with* BEN *and* CAMILLE *with* ALICE; *all ad-lib "Oops"-type remarks, and* CAMILLE *switches to dance with* BEN, *but* DON *stops just short of starting dance with* ALICE, *reacts to something, turns back and taps* BEN *on shoulder; MUSIC ceases abruptly;* BEN *and* CAMILLE *break clinch, stare at him apprehensively.*) You're not cutting in already—?!

DON. (*To* BEN, *ominously:*) What have you got in your pocket?!

BEN. Wh-what—?

DON. When we were dancing, I felt something in your pocket! I want to see it!

BEN. (*As* DON *deliberately reaches into* BEN'S *inner jacket pocket.*) Hey, hold on! Now, really, this is intolerable! I don't have to let you—uh—! (*Last syllable is because* DON *has pulled rubber chicken out of* BEN'S *pocket, and is holding it aloft in grim triumph.*)

DON. *Well—?!*

ALICE. Don, darling, don't jump to conclusions, I can explain—!

DON. Go ahead.

ALICE. (*Stares at him, then turns to* CAMILLE.) Tell him, Camille!

CAMILLE. (*Looking about room desperately for assistance.*) Uh—well—it's this way—you see— (*Sights lamp, rushes to pick it up, inspired.*) *This* is the reason you found that chicken!

BEN. There! See? You were upset about nothing.

DON. Hold it! What's that lamp got to do with this chicken?

CAMILLE. It's a party-theme! Magic! I bought this old lamp, and decided to build a party around it. So Ben brought the chicken—

ALICE. (*Catching the drift, speaking with shaky conviction:*) And I was going to bring that string of colored scarves, only I couldn't find them beause you'd already found them and taken them away, and— (*Stops as* DON *quietly takes revolver from inside jacket.*) I take it you don't believe me.

BEN. (*With no conviction at all.*) Maybe—maybe that's a *trick* gun—you know—to go with the party theme—?

CAMILLE. (*Clutching lamp to her breast.*) Don, are you crazy?! Put that gun away!

DON. (*To* ALICE *and* BEN, *not even hearing* CAMILLE, *with grim despondency:*) I walked and I walked, and I thought and I thought, and when I finally knew in my heart what was happening, I knew there was only one thing to do—! (*Points gun at* BEN.) Do you know what that one thing is—?

BEN. (*Trying not to cry.*) Don't I even get a blindfold? (DON *brings up bundled kerchiefs, offers them to* BEN, *on:*)

DON. Take your pick.

ALICE. (*Leaps between them leaning back against* BEN.) Don! No! Wait! Let me explain!

DON. (*Circling, trying to get a bead on* BEN, *who circles with* ALICE *in front of him, trying not to get beaded upon.*) Alice, get out of the way, or I'll shoot *anyhow! One! . . . Two! . . .*

CAMILLE. (*Jumping between* ALICE *and* DON, *and joining the circling.*) Don, this is ridiculous! Do you know how silly you look?!

ALICE. Especially with that chicken!

DON. (*Realizes he still holds chicken and kerchiefs in non-gun-hand, throws them impatiently into armchair, waves gun at group.*) Enough is enough! Get away from him, both of you, or I'll shoot right *through* you!

BEN. (*Crouching and circling desperately behind women.*) Don't listen to him! He's bluffing! I've heard that kind of bravado before!

DON. I'll show you who's bluffing! (*Fires gun straight up into air;* ALICE *and* CAMILLE *scream and diverge Right and Left, exposing* BEN—*now at extreme Upstage position between door and corridor—who gives a scream of his own, and—with incredible speed—opens wardrobe, jumps inside, and pulls door shut.*) You think *that's* going to save you, you wife-stealer—?! (*FIRES directly at wardrobe.*)

BEN. (*From wardrobe.*) Aaah! (DON *FIRES again.*) Aaah! (*And again.*) Aaah! (*Etcetera, over and over—shot-scream-shot-scream—during:*)

CAMILLE. (*As* ALICE *moans and faints into chair atop chicken and kerchiefs.*) *Oh,* I wish I'd never *given* this party! I wish I'd never moved *into* this apartment! I— (*Pauses as WIND begins to whistle loudly, looks at lamp, thrusts it out to stare at it at arm's length, as lights fade down to single-spot upon her and lamp.*) . . . Did you say something—?!

HOLLOW DISEMBODIED VOICE. (*Over WIND:*) Never moved into this apartment . . . never moved in . . . never moved in . . .

BLACKOUT

ACT ONE

SCENE 3

As in Scene 2, CLOCK STRIKES hour of eight, lights come up slowly to full brightness by end of striking. Setting is same as at start of Scene 1, except that the rubber chicken is on cocktail table, and the lamp on the taboret.

As scene begins, DOORBELL rings. After a moment, BEN *enters from corridor, in pajamas and slippers, and opens door to admit* CAMILLE, *carrying a large dress-box. She stops, stares.*

CAMILLE. Oh. Uh—you must be Ben. I'm Camille. Is Alice here?

BEN. (*Closing door.*) If I say no, will you be terrified?

CAMILLE. (*Looking him up and down.*) Probably. Though I do like your taste in pajamas.

ALICE. (*Off.*) Camille? Is that you?

CAMILLE. Yes, it is! What's going on here, anyhow?! I came as soon as you called.

ALICE. (*Off.*) Oh, it's a long stupid story! Ben, will you turn your back so I can come out?

BEN. Sure thing. (*Stations himself before bar, facing Downstage.*) Olee-olee-oshun-free!

ALICE. (*Emerges from corridor in panties and bra, takes box from* CAMILLE, *who reacts to her getup.*) Oh, thanks, Camille! I don't know what I'd have done without you! (*Exits into corridor with box.*)

CAMILLE. (*Looking from her to* BEN *and back.*) It looks like you've done *plenty* without me!

ALICE. (*Off.*) Now, really! If I had, would I make Ben turn his back?

CAMILLE. I thought that was for my benefit—not that it worked. I mean, him dressed like *that*—and you *un*dressed like that—!

ALICE. (*Off.*) Honestly, it's all quite innocent.

CAMILLE. Then why is this man in his pajamas?

BEN. Because it's my bedtime.

ALICE. (*Off.*) There, you see?

CAMILLE. No, I *don't* see. Did he put his pajamas on while *you* were in the bedroom?

BEN. (*Quite sincerely.*) It's all right. I kept my eyes closed.

CAMILLE. (*Reacts.*) *You* kept *your* eyes closed?! (*Calls Off to* ALICE:) You forgot to mention on the phone—exactly what *did* happen to your *own* clothes?

ALICE. (*Off.*) I got *egg yolk* all over them!

CAMILLE. (*To* BEN.) How did *that* happen?

BEN. A silly accident. Her hand slipped while she was breaking the egg into my hat.

CAMILLE. Why should she do a thing like that?!

ALICE. (*Off.*) Ben was teaching me some new tricks!

CAMILLE. (*Mis-sizing up situation.*) I'll *bet* he was!

BEN. I don't think you understand—

(*Stops as* ALICE *enters from corridor, dressed in a Scout Leader's uniform, including peaked "Mountie" hat with chinstrap.*)

ALICE. Camille! What were you *thinking* of? I can't go home in *this!*

CAMILLE. I'm sorry, Alice, but it was the only thing of mine that I thought would *fit* you! I must admit, it looks just great on you.

ALICE. But it's so inappropriate! What would *Don* say if he saw me in this?

CAMILLE. Isn't it a little late to worry about what Don might think?! I never thought you were the sort of wife who—

ALICE. But I'm not! I know this must look sort of odd—but Ben has been giving me lessons—

CAMILLE. Look, all I know is that you are married to one of the most insanely jealous men I have ever met, and tonight you call up and tell me you're in a man's apartment with no dress on, and—!

BEN. If you'll just let us explain—! (*Stops as DOORBELL rings, and loud KNOCKING sounds at door.*)

DON. (*Off. KNOCKING loudly between bursts of speech.*) Alice! . . . Open this door! . . . I know you're in there! . . .

ALICE. It's my husband!

CAMILLE. Oh, no!

BEN. How did he find us?!

CAMILLE. He must have followed me here!

DON. (*Off. More KNOCKING and DOORBELL-ringing amid.*) Alice, come out of there! . . . Are you going to unlock this door?! . . .

ALICE. Oh, dear, he mustn't find out what we've been doing!

CAMILLE. How're you gonna *stop* him?

ALICE. (*To* BEN.) Quick! Hide the chicken!

CAMILLE. The *chicken—?!*

BEN. (*Grabbing up chicken, waving it about.*) What'll I *do* with it?!

DON. (*Off. DOORBELL/KNOCKING as before.*) Alice! . . . *Alice!* . . . ALICE! . . . *ALICE!* . . .

ALICE. (*Overlapping* DON's *shouts, running toward door while gesturing for* BEN's *benefit.*) The window! Throw it out the window! Don mustn't know!

CAMILLE. (*As* BEN *dashes toward window—which he won't be able to open—and* ALICE *presses her back to the door along the crack of the doorknob-side, and* DON *continues to ad-lib shouts.*) Mustn't know *what?!*

BEN. I can't get the window up!

CAMILLE. (*Fluttery echo to* ALICE.) He can't get the window up!

DON. (*Off.*) I'm going to shoot off the lock! (*Before* ALICE *can even realize her spot, GUN FIRES, and with both hands on her rear, screaming loudly,* ALICE *gallops off down corridor, as* DON *bursts in, in overcoat and hat, waving revolver about like a madman, and* CAMILLE *screams in fear, and a panicky* BEN, *facing Upstage, hides chicken behind back.*) Where is she!? Where is she!?

CAMILLE. Don! Stop! Put that gun down! Listen to reason!

DON. (*Coming down toward her and* BEN, *step by ominous step.*) Don't try to protect her! Who's he? Is this the guy? What are you hiding there?

BEN. (*Backing Downstage Left, keeping chicken behind back.*) Now, look, fella—you have no reason to come busting in here like this—waving a gun around and scaring people—!

DON. Do you deny you're the man who's been secretly seeing my wife?!

BEN. Well, *no,* but—

DON. Do you deny she's been coming daily to this apartment?

BEN. Well, *no,* but—

DON. Do you deny I have every right to blast you into a million pieces—?!

CAMILLE. (*Whom* DON *has now passed in his stalking of* BEN.) Ben, don't answer that!

BEN. But I *do* deny it!

DON. (*Almost upon him.*) You coward! Why don't you admit the truth and die like a man?! And what the hell are you hiding from me?!

BEN. Oh—what's the use! (*Whips out chicken, holds it dangling before* DON'S *face.*) There!

DON. (*Takes it.*) *A rubber chicken—?!*

BEN. (*Turns away from him, facing out front.*) Now you know everything! (*Leans forward in resignation, hands resting upon lamp.*)

DON. (*Bewildered, turns to* CAMILLE, *holds up chicken.*) What's the meaning of this?!

CAMILLE. *You're* asking *me?!*

ALICE. (*Off.*) Ben—?

(DON *and* CAMILLE *look toward corridor, but* BEN *does not.*)

BEN. Yes?

ALICE. (*Off.*) Have you got any band-aids—?!

DON. That's Alice! What does she want band-aids for?

CAMILLE. You *shot* her when you blew the lock off the door, you maniac!

DON. Oh, no! (*Horrified, starts Upstage at a trot, calling.*) Alice, Alice darling—!

ALICE. (*Off. With grim resignation.*) It's all right, it's only a flesh wound!

DON. (*Now before wardrobe, stops, looks off Right down corridor, sags with remorse at what he sees, then starts off Right, on:*) Oh, darling, darling, what have I *done—?!* (*On final word, trips, just Upstage of bar, and revolver, still in his hand and pointed before him, FIRES, and we hear* ALICE *give a yelp of shock and displeasure;* DON *covers his eyes with one hand, mutters wearily.*) Oh, damn!

CAMILLE. (*Covers her face.*) Oh, boy!

BEN. (*Shuts his eyes.*) Oh, brother!

ALICE. (*Off. Very weakly, as others uncover and open eyes.*) It's all right . . . Don . . . I know you didn't mean it—! . . . If only—it didn't *hurt* so much. . . .

DON. (*Holds revolver up before face.*) Stupid gun! This is all *your* fault! (*Throws it to floor out of our view behind bar, and we hear it FIRE as it strikes;* DON *stares downward a moment, then turns out front, leaning hands on bar, a slow and quite exquisite agony blossoming upon his face, on:*) Oh-oh! Ooooo-baby! Ah-haaaaa! Wow!

(*And as* ALICE *continues to moan, off,* CAMILLE *again covers her face with her hands and starts to sob, and* DON'S *groans and facial agonies grow in volume and intensity,* BEN*—still leaning in stoic resignation on lamp—speaks softly.*)

BEN. Oh, I wish I'd never *become* a magician . . . I wish I'd never *met* Alice. . . . (*Whistle of WIND comes up slowly to top volume as lights start to fade on scene, but remain on* BEN *and lamp for a moment, as he stares in perplexity down at lamp, and says:*) Was it something I *said—?*

HOLLOW DISEMBODIED VOICE. (*Over WIND.*) Never became a magician . . . never met Alice . . . never a magician . . . never met Alice . . . *Okay,* Ben, if *that's* the way you *want* it . . . (*Gives demonic laugh.*)

BLACKOUT and CURTAIN

ACT TWO

SCENE 1

Darkness. Westminster-chimes go through sixteen-note melody, but when hour strikes eight, sound is made by cuckoo-clock, and lights do not come up until full eight cuckooings have sounded, and when lights come up, they do so instantly, rather than gradually.

We see setting same as at start of Act One, Scene 1, except that lamp is on taboret already, and armchairs are occupied: DON, *in shirtsleeves and slippers, sits reading newspaper color comics section in Right armchair;* CAMILLE, *in housecoat and slippers, is in Left armchair, knitting. When they speak,* CAMILLE *will use a middle-aged—almost a "granny"—squeak-voice, and* DON *will speak in illiterate-mountaineer tone, the voice of one who is not actually stupid but who nevertheless sounds that way.*

DON. (*After about two beats, lower paper.*) Ya know, Milly—

CAMILLE. (*Without looking up from knitting.*) Yes, Donald—?

DON. I been thinking . . .

CAMILLE. Oh, *good!* (*Continues to knit; after a moment,* DON *turns head her way.*)

DON. Dontcha wanna know about *what?*

CAMILLE. (*This hadn't occurred to her; she lowers knitting, stares out front, then finally turns to face him.*) Why . . . I guess so, Donald . . . if it will make you happy.

DON. You're a good wife, Milly.

CAMILLE. Aw, shucks! (*Returns to knitting, he returns to reading comics; after a moment, she lowers knitting, frowns, turns to him.*) Donald—?

DON. (*Lowers paper, turns blank look upon her.*) Yeah, Milly—?

CAMILLE. You never did tell me what you were thinking about. (*Pauses, frowns; then:*) *Did* you?

DON. By golly, I didn't!

CAMILLE. (*Relieved.*) That's what I thought! (*Returns to knitting, he returns to paper; then he lowers paper, turns to her again.*)

DON. Do you *wanna* hear it?

CAMILLE. (*Looks up, blank.*) Do I wanna hear *what?*

DON. What I been thinking about.

CAMILLE. Oh, sure.

DON. I been thinking about The Boy.

CAMILLE. What boy?

DON. Our boy.

CAMILLE. Oh, *that* boy.

DON. Yeah.

CAMILLE. That's nice. (*Almost returns to knitting, then stops, turns his way.*) *What've* you been thinking about The Boy?

DON. About how proud he's gonna make us.

CAMILLE. I'm proud right now.

DON. Oh, yeah, me too. But I mean when he finishes his schooling and all.

CAMILLE. I won't be no prouder than than I am right now.

DON. How come?

CAMILLE. *I* don't know.

DON. Oh. (*Pause, during which she continues to stare at him; then:*)

CAMILLE. Will *you* be?

DON. Will I be what?

CAMILLE. Prouder then than you are now?
DON. Well, sure!
CAMILLE. Oh. Well, then, I guess I will be, too.
DON. You're a good wife, Milly.
CAMILLE. I know.

(*Return to paper/knitting for an instant, then* DON *lowers paper, and she lowers knitting in anticipation of a remark.*)

DON. Milly?
CAMILLE. Yes, Donald?
DON. Where *is* The Boy?
CAMILLE. In his room, doing his book-learning. Like he is every night this time.
DON. How come he ain't out playing ball with the other kids?
CAMILLE. Now-now, Donald. You *know* he can't do that!
DON. But why not?
CAMILLE. For one thing, it's dark out.
DON. Oh. Oh, yeah, it is. But how about in the daytime?
CAMILLE. He's in school, then.
DON. Oh, yeah. (*Digests this; then:*) Don't he *never* get to play ball with the other kids?
CAMILLE. No.
DON. How come?
CAMILLE. What did *you* do when *you* were his age?
DON. I played ball with the other kids.
CAMILLE. *That's* how come!
DON. Oh, yeah. I forgot. (*Will fold paper and place it on table, during:*) That boy is gonna have all the things I never had when I was a boy.
CAMILLE. (*Sets knitting on table.*) Do you mean that, Donald?
DON. *Course* I mean it! . . . Why?

CAMILLE. He wants a bicycle for his birthday. Can he get it?

DON. No.

CAMILLE. Why not?

DON. I *had* a bicycle.

CAMILLE. Oh, yeah. I forgot.

DON. You're a good wife, Milly. (*Reaches for her hand, takes it; they smile at each other for a long stupid moment; then* BEN *enters via corridor, wearing thick glasses and short pants; he is skipping, and skips down to them, standing just above their handclasp.*)

BEN. Mummy, Daddy, I have completed my assigned scholastic tasks!

CAMILLE. Oh, *ain't* that pretty, Donald! I just love the way Ben-Boy talks!

DON. Yeah. Me, too. All them big words and all. Makes my head hurt just t' listen to him!

CAMILLE. But it surely is beautiful!

DON. It surely is. Wish I *understood* some of it, though.

CAMILLE. He said he was done with his book-learning.

DON. Gol-*ly!* I never would have suspicioned that! And you understood him!

CAMILLE. Oh, no, I don't understand hardly none of what he says no more.

DON. Then how'd you know he was done?

CAMILLE. 'Cause he *never* comes out till he's done.

DON. (*To* CAMILLE.) *Boy,* you are smart!

BEN. Thank you, Daddy. (*As* CAMILLE *and* DON *stare blankly at him, DOORBELL rings.*) Hark! I detect the imminent presence of a nocturnal visitation!

DON. Never mind your fancy talk! There's somebody at the door!

BEN. Shall I ascertain the newcomer's identity?

DON. No, just go see who it is.

CAMILLE. Oh, Donald, do you think he *should?*

DON. Why not? He's the closest.

CAMILLE. It's just—this *feeling* I have—this terrible feeling that whoever is at the door is gonna make some kind of difference to us all.

BEN. You are apprehensive about a potential alteration in the status quo?

DON. You watch your mouth in front o' your mother!

CAMILLE. Oh, Donald, don't take on. He didn't *mean* nothing by it! (*Fondly takes* BEN's *hand.*) *Did* you, Ben-Boy?!

BEN. But—Mummy—*everything* I say possesses significance.

DON. Any more o' that backtalk, you're gonna get the strap!

BEN. But Daddy—!

CAMILLE. Hush, now, botha you! Mustn' kill the boy's spirit, Donald. *I* don't mind a little sass. (*DOORBELL.*) Ben-Boy, ain't you never gonna get that door?

DON. That's your *mother* talking, boy! You get a *move* on, *hear?!*

BEN. I would be most amenable to acquiesce, Daddy, but Mummy still retains a purchase upon my metacarpal phalanges. (*Tugs slightly at her hand-grip to demonstrate.*)

DON. (*Stands.*) I'm gonna bust his mouth!

BEN. (*jerks free of grip, flings hands overhead in vast shrug.*) All *right,* already, I'll answer the door!

CAMILLE. (*As* BEN *goes to door, and* DON *re-sits in huffy triumph.*) I admire the way you put him in his place, Donald.

DON. A man's gotta do what a man's gotta do!

(*As* DON *and* CAMILLE *settle back in chairs, smugly righteous,* BEN *opens door and* ALICE *enters; she is in a red-slit-sequined dress, hands on hips, eyes narrowed in sultry fashion, and is obviously a vamp on the prowl.*)

ALICE. (*As* BEN *gawks at her, in open-mouthed fascination, she will speak—and continue to speak, no matter what happens—like a reincarnation of Early Mae West.*) Hi there, Big Boy!

BEN. (*Takes both her hands eagerly, as he corrects her:*) "*Ben*-Boy" . . .

ALICE. Down, boy! (*He hastily releases her hands.*) I'm your new neighbor, just across the hall—you lucky fool!

BEN. Gol-*ly!* . . . Is there—something I can *do* for you—?

ALICE. (*Looks him slowly up and down before replying.*) I'm not sure. But I just love surprises!

BEN. Gol-*ly!*

ALICE. None of that sweet-talk, you silver-tongued devil, you!

CAMILLE. (*Since neither she nor* DON *has looked Upstage at all.*) Who was at the door, darling?

BEN. (*Eyes still locked upon* ALICE, *swallows, then manages:*) It's our new neighbor-lady!

DON. Well, find out what she *wants.*

BEN. (*With nervous smile.*) I think I *know* what she wants!

CAMILLE. Oh, good.

ALICE. (*To* BEN.) Don't be to sure o' yourself. I know what I want—but how do I know you can get it for me?

BEN. I'll sure do my dangedest!

ALICE. Good. Good.

BEN. (*Swallows; then:*) Uh— What *do* you want?

ALICE. I wonder if I could borrow a rubber chicken—?!

BEN. A *what?*

ALICE. A *chicken.*

BEN. (*Blank.*) A *what?*

ALICE. *You* know— A gallinaceous fowl of the domesticated barnyard variety?

BEN. Oh, well, why didn't you *say* so! Sure, we've got one.

ALICE. You have?

BEN. Hasn't everybody?

ALICE. Good. Good. (*Starts out still-open door, pauses on threshold for:*) I'll be over at—*my* place. Get the chicken. My door will be open. Then, any time you're ready—just—come across! (*Saunters out, leaving door open.*)

BEN. (*Staring saucer-eyed after her.*) Yes, *ma'am!* Gol-*ly!* (*Smacks one fist decisively into opposing palm, dashes madly off down corridor;* DON *and* CAMILLE *sit silently for a moment or two; then:*)

DON. Did you hear that, Milly?

CAMILLE. I surely did!

DON. The Boy has found himself a Painted Woman. There go all our hopes for him. All our plans. All our dreams.

CAMILLE. Even our rubber chicken.

DON. (*Stands.*) There's only one thing to do.

CAMILLE. I understand, Donald. (DON *goes Upstage, exits into corridor; after a moment, we hear a GUNSHOT;* CAMILLE *sighs, picks up her knitting, and is wearily going at it when* DON *enters slowly, his manner slumped and depleted, then faces Downstage while still Upstage of bar;* CAMILLE *senses him, pauses in her knitting, and speaks without turning her head.*) Is it over?

DON. All over, Milly.

CAMILLE. I suppose—now—you'll have to go tell someone what you did, Donald.

DON. (*Nods.*) That's my plan, Milly.

CAMILLE. (*Resumes knitting.*) I'll miss you, Donald.

DON. A man's gotta do what a man's gotta do. And what I gotta do— (*Looks off Left through still-open door, smiles, moistens fingertips of both hands on tongue, slicks back hair at temples, lifts rubber chicken into view from behind bar, and marches gleefully off through open door, holding chicken by neck and out before him, as one might carry a precious gift, his eyes dancing with amorous anticipation, on:*) is go out there and *surrender* myself! (*He is off; then we hear him croon in a happy singsong voice.*) Oh, neigh-bor la-dy—! I've brought you a pres-ent . . . !

ALICE. (*Off.*) What kind of present, Big Boy?

DON. (*Off.*) It's a little *fowl!*

ALICE. (*Off.*) Good. Good. C'mon in!

CAMILLE. (*Has listened to this, sighs, sets knitting down on table, rises, comes down to lamp, during:*) Guess I'll pick up old Granny Carstairs' heirloom lamp, and start in walkin' over the hill t' the poor-house . . . (*Picks up lamp, stares wistfully out front.*) It's all the fault o' this-here modrin society where everyone's lives get all soggy from weepin' and wailin'. How I wish there was someplace we could go to *not* get soggy. . . . (*WIND begins to whistle loudly; she stares at lamp as lights begin to dim to a single spot on her and lamp.*) Gol-*ly*—!

HOLLOW DISEMBODIED VOICE. (*Over WIND.*) . . . to *not* get soggy . . . to *not* guess soggy . . . to *not* guess *socky* . . . Nagasaki . . . *Nagasaki!* . . . Nagasaki-Nagasaki-Nagasaki-Nagasaki— (*Now that word-repeat sounds like steam engine, sound is capped by TRAIN WHISTLE as we go into:*)

BLACKOUT

ACT TWO

SCENE 2

In darkness, we hear the sixteen-note Westminster-chime melody, but the hour of eight strikes upon a deep, sonorous oriental gong, lights coming up at moderate speed while last gong-stroke is still reverberating. Stage is set as at top of show, except that lamp is on taboret, and taboret is set dead center on top of cocktail table. ALICE, *in colorful kimono, is seated tailor-fashion on floor in front of table, facing Downstage, and playing something mournful on a flute. [NOTE: Throughout scene, characters will speak with mock-Japanese singsong inflection and pronunciation, and their movements will all be in quick short-step shuffles, and when they have nothing to do with their hands, they will carry them clasped against their chests, and their heads whenever possible will be held tilted bird-like to Right or Left.] A few moments after lights are up, we hear a loud GONG.*

ALICE. (*Ceases playing flute, looks out front.*) Ah! Is doorbell! I get! (*Rises, shuffles daintily to front door, opens it to admit* CAMILLE, *also in kimono; shuffles backward a bit and bows.*) Ah-so! Is my good friend, Milly-San! (*Actually, pronunciation is closer to ". . . good fliend, Mirry-San" but there will be no attempt to cover all the "L"—"R" switches in the dialogue, except where important.*)

CAMILLE. (*Bows, also.*) This humble one is honored to enter house of friend Alice-San.

ALICE. No-no. Honor is all mine, Milly-San. (*Bows.*)

CAMILLE. Ah, no, *this* one have all honor. (*Bows.*)

ALICE. You wanna fight, we be here all day! How about half-honor for you, half-honor for me?

CAMILLE. (*Bows.*) Okay. We sprit diffelence! (*Shuffles Down Left of armchairs as* ALICE *closes door.*)

ALICE. (*Door shut, will shuffle Down to Right of armchairs, so that she faces* CAMILLE *across table, before speaking; then:*) How you rike new shline?

CAMILLE. (*Observing lamp/taboret combo.*) It does honor to ashes of honorable ancestor inside lovely urn. It has beauty like moon rising over Fujiyama. It sings in heart like small bird among leaves of emerald. It glows like golden sun that sets upon purple sea while white waves beat upon copper sands—

ALICE. Arr *light,* arleady! Why you just not say shline velly pletty and let go at that, okay?!

CAMILLE. I sorry, Alice-San. (*Bows.*)

ALICE. You forgiven, Milly-San. (*Bows.*)

CAMILLE. You good kid, Al. (*Bows.*)

ALICE. You too, Mil. (*Bows.*)

CAMILLE. Not good as *you,* kid. (*Bows.*)

ALICE. Arr light, arr light! (*Both straighten; then:*) Now we get down to business, okay?

CAMILLE. Where is tea?

ALICE. What tea?

CAMILLE. For business, always drink tea.

ALICE. I no make tea. Tea ceremony are for *money*-business; I call you here to talk of *monkey*-business.

CAMILLE. Ah-so! You gonna go door-to-door, sell monkeys?

ALICE. Sometime, Milly-San, this one think you no got head on rightside up. I talk about *other* kind monkey-business!

CAMILLE. This humble one begs pardon. (*Bows.*)

ALICE. You forgiven. (*Bows.*)

CAMILLE. You good kid. (*Bows.*)

ALICE. Enough, arleady! You leady to risten to me?

CAMILLE. This one leady. Tell Milly-San how Alice-San get into monkey business.

ALICE. (*Bows, then faces out front, holds flute up.*) One day, I sit on back porch, and pray on my frute!

CAMILLE. Ah-so?

ALICE. Suddenly, hear man say, "Hey, kiddo, you pray a mean frute!"

CAMILLE. Was man Alice-San's husband?

ALICE. Do not be silly, Milly. Beloved husband of Alice-San have honorable tin ear.

CAMILLE. Ah-so! So tell this humble one about man on porch.

ALICE. Man has name of Ben-San!

CAMILLE. (*Fingertips on cheeks, rocks head Left-Right-Left.*) Oh! Oh! Oh!

ALICE. You know of this man?

CAMILLE. Who does not? Ben-San is known around town as absorute recher!

ALICE. Alice-San knows this.

CAMILLE. And Alice-San does not care?

ALICE. Oh, yes, Alice-San care. But heart of Alice-San will not risten to leason!

CAMILLE. Ah-so! So what you do *now?*

ALICE. I tell truth to honorable husband, Don-San.

CAMILLE. Don-San gonna get mad.

ALICE. Ret him! This humble one can not go on rivving a rie! (*GONG.*) Ah-so! That will be Ben-San!

CAMILLE. How you know?

ALICE. I lecognize his ling! (*Shuffles to door, admits* BEN, *also in kimono, which is belted with the colored stage-magician scarves.*) Ben-San! You have allived at rast!

BEN. (*Bows.*) Alice-San's words are as true as Alice-San is beautifur. (*Goes to kiss her.*)

ALICE. (*Pulls slightly away, indicates* CAMILLE.) Oh, not! Not! We are not arone!

BEN. (*Looks down to* CAMILLE.) Ah-so! And who is this ruvry brossom?

CAMILLE. This one has honor to be Milly-San, o Ben-San. (*Bows.*)

BEN. (*Comes down to her while* ALICE *closes door.*) Ah, then you have heard of this one!

CAMILLE. Ownry that you are rousy recher.

BEN. Do not brame me for ruvving Alice-San. She ensraved me when she prayed on her frute!

ALICE. (*Coming Down to them.*) Do not speak so roud, ruvver! You will waken Don-San!

CAMILLE. Alice-San's husband is in the *house?!*

ALICE. It is arr light. He is asreep in his loom!

DON. (*Shuffles dramatically into view above bar, also in kimono.*) This is not so!

ALICE. Don-San!

DON. Ah-so!

BEN. Oh, no!

CAMILLE. (*Brief shuffle toward front door.*) This one go!

DON. (*Shuffling after her, the two moving in childish choo-choo fashion.*) Not so fast, Milly-San! You are important witness!

CAMILLE. (*Stops.*) Witness to what?

DON. To dishonor upon house of Don-San! (*Shuffles back to confront* ALICE.) Alice-San, what you have to say for yourself?! Have my honorable ears heard the tellible tluth?

ALICE. Yes! Is tlue! I have taken Ben-San as ruvver!

DON. But Ben-San is rousy recher!

ALICE. Ben-San may be rousy recher, but he is ruvry ruvver!

DON. Ownry husband should be ruvver!

ALICE. Husband's words are tlue, but there is tellible plobrem!

CAMILLE and BEN. What *is* plobrem?!

ALICE. As ruvver, Don-San is absorute frop!

DON. Who you corring a frop?!

ALICE. Not just prain frop. *Lotten* frop!

DON. (*Covers face with hands.*) Oh, shame! Shame! Shame! Shame has come upon house of Don-San!

ALICE. Is your own faurt!

DON. (*Uncovers face, stares at her.*) *My* faurt? How you figure? You are ruvvers with absorute recher, and now you say shame on house is *my* faurt? How come you say that?

ALICE. Who arways sreep arr day in bedloom?

DON. This one.

ALICE. Who teach me to pray on frute?

DON. This one.

ALICE. Who is lotten frop as ruvver?

DON. This one?

ALICE. You said it!

DON. (*Palms to temples.*) Ah! Ah! Ah! Alice-San, you have hurt this one, deepry! There is no more honor in my house! How I show face at office? How I even order *dlink* in *saroon?* Arr is rost! (*Drops hands to sides.*) This one go to bedloom, take honorable rife!

ALICE. Ah, no! Do not do such thing! Stop! (*Takes his sleeve.*)

DON. (*Frowns, gently removes her fingers from his sleeve.*) How many times I terr you: *Don't stop me if you've hurt this one?!* (*Bows to group, they bow back to him.*) This one go now, save honor of house by ending dishonored rife! (*Starts off.*)

BEN. (*Starts after him.*) Wait, Don-San! This one go arong, to catch your forring body when you end dishonored rite!

DON. Ben-San would do that for Don-San?

BEN. Even rousy recher knows how to be porite!

(DON *and* BEN *shuffle off down corridor;* CAMILLE *and* ALICE *stand and wait, Upstage hands cupped to Upstage ears; we hear a GUNSHOT Offstage; they fold hands and bow heads; after a moment,* DON *re-enters, smiling inscrutably, holding pistol; the women sense his presence, look up at him in surprise.*)

DON. (*Shrugs.*) I miss.

ALICE. (*Gives little scream of dismay, shuffles rapidly up to him, takes pistol, holds it to temple, and while holding it there, shuffles past him and out down corridor, on:*) Oh! Ruvver! Ruvver! Ruvver! Ruvver! Ruvver! . . . (*A moment later, off, we hear second GUNSHOT.*) Ah-so! (*We hear THUD, off.*)

DON. (*Rests hands upon lamp.*) All is honor once more! Have saved honorable ancestors from shame! I so grad we are rivving in civirized countly! This one would sure like to see how situation could have been handered any diffelently! (*Then he and* CAMILLE *stare at lamp as WIND whistles.*) . . . What the *herr—?!*

HOLLOW DISEMBODIED VOICE. (*Over WIND.*) . . . this situation . . . handled differently . . . handled differently . . . handled differently . . .

BRACKOUT

ACT TWO

SCENE 3

Same bit with darkness, sixteen-note melody, but this time the eight-stroke indication of the hour is made by eight short bursts on a police whistle, as lights come up slowly. When we see Stage, taboret will be gone; lamp is atop bar; DON, *now in suit and fedora, is pacing back and forth in Downstage Left area, hands clasped behind back. After a moment or two, we hear a loud KNOCKING at front door.* DON *hurries Upstage to yank door open, but he suddenly hesitates, right hand going ominously inside left breast of jacket, left hand on knob.*

DON. Who is it?

CAMILLE. (*Off.*) It's me, you lunkhead! Open the damn door!

DON. (*Relaxes, wipes sweat from brow, then pulls door open;* BEN, *with eyes terrified, and a gag of those colored scarves over his mouth, and his wrists and ankles roped together, comes hopping in, followed by a gum-chewing* CAMILLE, *dressed in mink coat and Empress Eugenie hat with short veil, and holding a revolver pointed at* BEN'*s back.*) Oh, good, you got him!

CAMILLE. (*As she and* DON *each take* BEN *by an arm, and help him hop Down to Left armchair, where they will fling him down.*) Yeah, and it wasn't easy, neither! You never *saw* so many cops on guard! The front door, the stairs, the apartment door, even the bedroom where they were keeping him incommunicado!

DON. It must've been tough getting to him!

CAMILLE. It sure was! I damn near ran out of bribes! (BEN, *now slumped in armchair, makes incoherent angry sounds through gag.*) I think Baffling Benjy wants to talk!

DON. Of course he wants to talk! If he didn't want to talk, we wouldn't have had to grab him!

CAMILLE. Well, I guess you can take the gag off him now. I just didn't want him saying the wrong thing to anybody on the bus ride over here.

DON. (*Slaps her.*) I told you to take a cab!

CAMILLE. I couldn't afford it! I used most of my money bribing policemen!

DON. Well, I guess it's safe enough now. (*Pulls gag down from* BEN'S *mouth so it dangles around his neck.*) Okay, squealer! What've you got to say for yourself?!

BEN. (*Makes same incoherent sounds as when gagged;* DON *smacks his face to snap him out of it; then:*) I ain't saying nothing till I see my mouthpiece, Mister Frisby!

DON. That's fair enough. (*Gets lamp from bar, holds it before* BEN, *lifts lid.*)

BEN. (*Peering into cavity.*) What's this?

CAMILLE. That's what's left of your mouthpiece!

BEN. (*Looks up at* DON.) You're putting me on! There's nothing in there but a pair of busted eyeglasses!

DON. Look again! (*When* BEN *peers inside once more:*) Well?

BEN. (*Looks up.*) What are those ten little shiny flat things?

DON. Fingernails! (*He and* CAMILLE *laugh in fiendish unison; then he replaces lid on lamp, starts back for bar with it.*)

BEN. (*Conversationally, to* CAMILLE.) How come no toenails?

CAMILLE. They wouldn't come outa the cement!

BEN. Poor Mister Frisby . . . !

DON. (*Putting lamp onto bar and starting back to* BEN.) Well, you know how *Alice* gets when our guests insist on being stubborn!

BEN. *Alice?! You* didn't turn little Mister Frisby over to *Awful Alice?!* He was so sweet, so harmless, so nice—!

CAMILLE. Funny, that's just what Awful Alice said about him.

DON. Yeah, she said working him over was a real pleasure.

CAMILLE. He never swore—

DON. He never cussed—

DON and CAMILLE. (*Leaning ominously over* BEN, *speaking with relish:*) He just *whimpered* a lot! (*Both laugh fiendishly, as* BEN *cowers.*)

BEN. (*As bravely as he can manage.*) Well—you're never going to get *me* to talk!

DON. Oh, *I* wouldn't *think* of it!

CAMILLE. *We'd* never lay a *finger* on you!

DON and CAMILLE. (*As* BEN *relaxes a bit, lean over him again for:*) We'll let *Alice* try to coax you into cooperating!

BEN. (*Waits till they are through laughing fiendishly again; then:*) You wouldn't!

CAMILLE. Oh, wouldn't we!

BEN. You can't!

DON. Oh, can't we!

BEN. You mustn't!

DON and CAMILLE. Why mustn't we?

BEN. Well, for one thing, Dirty Don—I'm your own brother!

DON. So how come that didn't keep you from squealing to the cops?!

BEN. That's different. It was my civic obligation to the community.

CAMILLE. (*Slaps him.*) You watch your language!

BEN. I'm sorry, Sis.

DON. Aw, enough of this messing around! Let's get Alice in here!

CAMILLE. Good idea! (*Places both pinky-fingers in mouth, blows once, then again, but no whistle;* BEN *chuckles scornfully; instantly,* CAMILLE *whips a pistol out of her pocket and holds it to his temple, and just as instantly* BEN *turns head toward kitchen and whistles shrilly; then* CAMILLE *calls:*) *Hey, Al-lussss—!*

ALICE. (*Off.*) Whaddaya want?!

DON. Move your tail in here, we've got another customer!

ALICE. (*Strides in from corridor, swivels to a stop facing down.*) Oh, good, I was getting bored!

CAMILLE. Did you bring your equipment?

ALICE. (*One palm to nape of neck, other palm against hip.*) Look for yourself!

DON. The *other* equipment, stupid!

ALICE. Oh, *that!* Sure! (*Lifts small violin-case from behind bar, saunters Down between armchairs to place it upon table.*) Hi, there, Baffling Benjy, how's tricks?!

BEN. Do your worst, Awful Alice. You'll never make me talk!

ALICE. We'll see about that! (*Opens case, goes to reach inside, then hesitantly flicks a glance at* BEN, *and then turns to* DON *for:*) Are you sure he can't get loose? I hate it when they wiggle.

DON. Don't worry about *that,* Alice. Crumby Camille tied those knots!

CAMILLE. It would take a *magician* to get outa them!

ALICE. Hey, ain't you forgetting something! Baffling Benjy-baby *is* a magician!

DON. Awful Alice is *right,* Crumby Camille! That's what all this ruckus is *about!* Benjy made Big Louie disappear from his cell just before the grand jury investigation on organized crime! That's why the cops were holding Benjy in the first place! They want to know what Benjy did with Big Louie so they can find him and arrest him, we want to know what Benjy did with Big Louie so we can find him and get him outa town!

CAMILLE. (*Drops out of character, addresses audience directly:*) Did you *get* all that? (*Smiles, satisfied, returns to playing scene.*)

DON. Who the hell were you talking to? (*Looks Left and Right at audience in blank bewilderment.*)

ALICE. Aw, don't mind Crumby Camille. She's cracked in the head!

CAMILLE. And who *put* the crack in it?!

ALICE. You *deserved* it!

CAMILLE. (*Leans across* BEN.) You take that back!

ALICE. (*Dangerously leans nose-to-nose with her across* BEN.) And what if I *won't* take that back?

CAMILLE. (*Wilting, shrugs matter-of-factly.*) Then *I'll* keep it.

DON. Will you two stop your jawing so Alice can get on with the torture?!

BEN. (*Leans forward between the nose-to-nose women bridging his chair at either side.*) Aw, let 'em jaw a little!

ALICE. Dirty Don is right. I've got work to do!

CAMILLE. Do I have to watch? I mean, Benjy's my own brother—!

DON. Yeah, that's right. . . . Tell you what, let's go out in the kitchen and have us a sandwich!

CAMILLE. Good idea! (*As they start toward corridor, to* BEN:) Now, don't scream too loud—you know it upsets my digestion! (DON *and* CAMILLE *exit, laughing fiendishly.*)

ALICE. (*Rummages in violin case.*) Now, let me see. . . . How shall I begin—?!

BEN. I may as well warn you, Awful Alice, I've been tortured before and I never talk!

ALICE. (*Glances up at him.*) How come?

BEN. (*Unhappily.*) I faint a lot.

ALICE. (*Back to rummaging in case.*) Well, don't worry, I'll do this nice and easy. Maybe you'll *wish* you could faint, but I won't go quite that far. . . . Ah! (*Lifts pair of pliers from case.*) I think I'll start by removing your toenails!

BEN. It's been done. And I still didn't talk.

ALICE. Okay, then, I'll start by cracking your knuckles—the permanent way!

BEN. It's been done. And I still didn't talk.

ALICE. Hmmmm! (*Scowling, drops pliers back into case, probes inside case a bit more, then her face suddenly brightens.*) Ah-ha! I've got it! There's *one* torture that *nobody* has ever been able to stand, never!

BEN. Alice! You don't mean—?!

ALICE. (*Pulls rubber chicken out of case, holds it aloft in sadistic triumph.*) Oh, but I *do!*

BEN. (*Hysterical with fear.*) No! No! Not the rubber chicken! You wouldn't be so inhuman!

ALICE. (*Menacing him with chicken, swinging back and forth by its neck from her hand, just before his wide-eyed face.*) And why wouldn't I—?!

BEN. Alice, how can you?! After all we've been to one another! Remember the moonlight . . . the flowers . . . the candy . . . the warmth of my arms . . . the touch of my lips?!

ALICE. (*Wavering.*) Stop it! Stop it, do you hear?! I've got a job to do! If *I* don't use this rubber chicken on *you,* the *rest* of the mob'll use it on *me!*

BEN. Oh, please! Think back! Those lazy walks in the autumn afternoon, the way you said my hair looks in the noonday sun— (ALICE *is definitely weakening now.*) that unforgettable night in Poughkeepsie!— Uh— I mean Schenectady!

ALICE. (*Frowns, looks suspiciously at him.*) "Schenectady"?

BEN. (*Hopefully.*) Hackensack—? No, that wasn't *you,* was it! (*Seeing her look.*) I guess not. But—what about all the *rest* of it?!

ALICE. The hell with it! I got work to do! (*Brings back chicken preparatory to swinging it into his face.*)

BEN. (*Shrieks in terror.*) No! Wait! There's something you should know!

ALICE. (*Pauses.*) What?

BEN. Lean closer! I don't want the others to hear . . . !

ALICE. (*Curiosity getting the better of her, leans close.*) Okay, Benjy-baby. What?

BEN. *This!* (*He has dropped rope from his wrists, and now grips hers with one hand, her mouth with the other, and stands, the other rope dropping away from his ankles.*) They don't call me Baffling Benjy for nothing! (*Starts to edge backwards toward door, towing her along.*) Not a sound, or you're a dead woman! (*Whirls suddenly,* ALICE *twirled around in front of him to face corridor, as he now does, because* DON *and* CAMILLE *have just stepped in, and* CAMILLE *has revolver trained on* BEN.)

CAMILLE. Okay, Benjy, back in the chair!

BEN. Not on your life! I'm getting out of here!

DON. Stop him, Crumby!

BEN. (*As* CAMILLE *brings up gun to fire.*) No you don't! (*Holds* ALICE *before him, continues to edge toward door.*) Not while I'm using Awful Alice as a shield!

CAMILLE. That's what *you* think! (*Gun FIRES;* ALICE *squeaks, slumps in* BEN'S *arms; he sets her untidily sagging across arm of nearest chair.*)

BEN. Well, thanks anyway, Alice.

ALICE. (*Lifts her head for last gasp.*) My pleasure. (*Slumps dead.*)

BEN. (*Raises hands, defeated.*) Okay. I'll tell you everything you want to know. Now that Alice is gone, nothing much matters anymore.

DON. Oh, yeah? (*Grabs revolver from* CAMILLE.) Gimme that gun! (*Trains it on* BEN.) You fool! *I* never cared what happened to Big Louie! All I cared about was Alice! I wanted her to get rid of you so I could have her all to myself! Yeah, that's right! All our lives, it's been nothing but one sibling rivalry after another! And now, the only woman I'll ever love is dead, do you hear, *dead,* and it's all your stinking fault!

CAMILLE. (*Directly to audience, as before:*) Did you *get* all that?

DON. Shut up!

CAMILLE. (*Back in character.*) Sorry.

BEN. Okay. Okay, Don. Go ahead and shoot. But I warn you— (*Takes step nearer to* DON.) no matter how many bullets you pump into me— (*Takes another step nearer.*) nothing is going to stop me from taking that neck of yours between my bare hands and strangling the evil life out of you—! (DON *brings up revolver and FIRES;* BEN *instantly sags, leaning gasping against bar.*) On the other hand— (DON *lets the revolver FIRE again into* BEN's *back;* BEN *jerks, then rasps:*) Wait! I got checks! I was only kidding! (*Clutches lamp to his chest, collapses onto floor.*)

DON. (*Comes out, stands over him, points revolver.*) And here comes one for the road!

CAMILLE. (*Lays hand on his arm.*) Dirty Don, wait! Haven't you done enough?!

DON. Well. . . . Maybe you're right. After all, he *is* my brother! (*Lowers revolver, starts off arm-in-arm with* CAMILLE.) Now, how about that sandwich?!

CAMILLE. Sounds super! (*They exit toward kitchen.*)

BEN. (*Lifts head weakly, still clutching lamp.*) Oh, how I wish Don hadn't been so jealous! That's what did all of this, his insane jealously! I wish we'd had another chance, somewhere, to be really good friends, to have him never show a speck of jealousy, to all behave ourselves with good manners and proper decorum, and— (*WIND begins to whistle; he thrusts lamp forward to stare at it from arm's length, on:*) Did you *get* all that—?!

HOLLOW DISEMBODIED VOICE. (*Over WIND.*) . . . good friends . . . never show jealously . . . behave ourselves . . . good manners . . . proper decorum . . . good manners . . . decorum . . .

BLACKOUT

ACT TWO

SCENE 4

Darkness, sixteen-note melody, and this time the eight chimes of the hour are deep, booming churchbell-volume sounds. Lights come up during final reverberation to reveal DON *standing at Downstage Left before taboret, now back in place with lamp on it,* BEN *standing at Right Center Stage near phonograph,* ALICE *standing before Left armchair, and* CAMILLE *standing just behind Right armchair. All hold a stemmed goblet in left hand, but have right hand behind back;* WOMEN *wear tiaras,* MEN *have monocles on cords in right eyes; all face out front, and remain in place, standing bright, crisp-toned, and stiff-upper-lippish, never looking at one another when they speak. As lights finally come up full, all take sip of drink in unison, lower glasses, take breath, and sigh. Then:*

CAMILLE. I say, this is jolly fun, what?

ALICE. Decidedly!

BEN. Right-o!

DON. Quite. (*All do same sip-sigh business in unison again; then:*) I say, Benjamin—?

BEN. Yes, your lordship?

DON. I was at the club the other day—

ALICE. Oh, how nice for you, darling.
DON. Ah, but it wasn't nice.
CAMILLE. Oh, how tiresome for you, my dear.
DON. Ah, but it wasn't tiresome, either.
BEN. Oh, good show!
ALICE. Quite. (*All sip-sigh, etc.; then:*)
DON. There is somewhat more to my story, you know.
BEN. Oh, really?
CAMILLE. How positively ripping!
ALICE. *Do* go on, Ducks!
DON. It seems the other members were all talking about Benjamin.
CAMILLE. What, *all?*
DON. Yes, all.
BEN. Every one?
DON. Every blasted one.
ALICE. Without exception?
DON. Absolutely.
CAMILLE. Strange . . .
BEN. Odd . . .
ALICE. Unusual . . . (*Sip-sigh business; then:*)
DON. Would you care to hear what they were *saying* about him? (ALICE *and* BEN *move heads for a fractional moment, to glance uneasily at one another, then face forward again.*)
BEN. Not especially.
ALICE. No.
CAMILLE. Oh, *I* would! Tell us, Sir Donald. Do.
DON. Very well. I shall.
ALICE. But, darling— I don't think—
BEN. Really—there's no need—
CAMILLE. Nonsense, let him speak! Sir Donald—?
DON. Thank you, Lady Camilla. (*Sip-sigh; then:*) They said that Benjamin was in the throes of an amorous liaison.
BEN. Ha-ha! Ridiculous!
ALICE. Ha-ha! What utter rot!

CAMILLE. Ha-ha! Of *course* it is! (*Sip-sigh; then:*) But *do* go on—!

DON. Would you all care to know with *whom?*

BEN. I'm dashed if *I* would!

ALICE. Nor I!

CAMILLE. It *is* absolutely vile—but I simply *must* know! With whom, Sir Donald?

DON. The woman they named was my own wife—Lady Alicia!

CAMILLE. What effrontery!

ALICE. What rubbish!

BEN. What balderdash! (*All do sip-sigh; then:*) I say . . . Sir Donald . . . if it *were* true—

ALICE. Benjamin, what are you saying?!

CAMILLE. Luv-a-*duck,* Benjamin, *yes?!*

BEN. I only say *"if"* it were.

DON. You mean—mere conjecture?

BEN. Oh, the *merest!*

ALICE. The *very* merest!

DON. Well, in that case—

CAMILLE. Yes, Sir Donald—?

BEN. Yes, your lordship—?

ALICE. Yes, darling—?

DON. I would call it a decidedly sticky wicket! (*All sip-sigh; then:*)

BEN. I say—is that *all* you would do—?

ALICE. If it *were* true, that is?

CAMILLE. My dears, what *else* could he do? After all, he is a member of the peerage!

DON. Quite.

CAMILLE. A knight of the realm!

DON. Quite.

CAMILLE. He would always keep a stiff upper lip and bite the bullet.

DON. Not quite.

ALICE. Ah?

BEN. Oh?

CAMILLE. Mmm?

DON. I should certainly gnash my teeth a bit. (*All sip-sigh; then:*) You must certainly grant me *that* much emotion!

CAMILLE. It is the very least we can do.

ALICE. Pip-pip!

BEN. Oh, ra-ther! (*All raise glasses to sip, but stop short of mouths, on:*)

DON. I say, Benjamin—? (*All lower glasses; then:*)

BEN. Yes, your lordship?

DON. *Is* it true? (BEN *and* ALICE *exchange another quick look; then:*)

BEN. I'm afraid so, your lordship.

DON. I see. (*All except* ALICE *sip-sigh; then:*)

ALICE. Darling—

DON. Yes, my love?

ALICE. Is that—*it?*

DON. Certainly.

ALICE. No tears, no rages, no loss of control?

DON. Certainly not, my dear. After all, I *am* an Englishman.

BEN. Hear-hear!

CAMILLE. Well spoken!

ALICE. Oh, but how dreadful!

DON. Dreadful?

ALICE. Yes, dreadful! To know that you do not even *care* that I love another!

DON. Ah, but Alicia, love, I *do* care.

ALICE. I refuse to believe that!

DON. Oh, dash it all, you *must* believe it!

ALICE. But how *can* I, when you just stand there and do nothing?!

CAMILLE. It *does* present a difficulty, Sir Donald.

BEN. Yes, I can scarce credit your contention, myself!

DON. I see. (*All do sip-sigh; then:*) Well, then, I daresay there's but one course open to me . . . (*Pulls revolver from inside left interior of jacket, FIRES back toward* BEN *without looking, re-pockets revolver during:)*

BEN. (*Whose monocle has popped free to dangle from cord at gunshot.*) Oh, I say! (*Sprawls flat on his back on floor.*)

ALICE. Why, darling—you *do* care!

DON. (*Leans now-empty gun-hand upon lamp, for:*) But of course I do! Still and all— How I wish I *didn't!* (*WIND starts; he looks down toward lamp as lights dim to pinspot on him.*) *Blimey!* (*Wind rises as we go into:*)

HOLLOW DISEMBODIED VOICE. (*Over WIND:*) . . . didn't care . . . didn't care . . . *didn't care* . . . (*WIND up full volume as we have:*)

BLACKOUT and CURTAIN

ACT THREE

Curtain rises in darkness. We hear WIND, and over it:

HOLLOW DISEMBODIED VOICE. How I wish I didn't care . . . didn't care . . . didn't care . . .

(*WIND and* VOICE *fade, and then in darkness we hear Westminster-chime melody. Strike of eight o'clock, this time, is eight equally spaced hen-clucks. Lights come up full immediately after last cluck. Setting is as at top of show, except that lamp is on taboret, and large bowl of fruit is centered on cocktail table.* ALICE *is seated in Left armchair, weeping, dabbing at eyes with small kerchief. DOORBELL rings. She hastily dries eyes, tucks kerchief into bosom of dress, answers door.* BEN *steps in, takes her hands.*)

BEN. Alice!

ALICE. Ben! I wasn't sure you'd come!

BEN. I ran all the way!

ALICE. (*Releases his hands, shuts door.*) I *had* to talk to *someone.*

BEN. (*With rugged male kindness, slightly out front.*) I understand. (*Follows her as she leads way to armchairs, where she will sit Left again, and he will sit Right.*) Tell me all about it.

ALICE. It's Don, Ben. He—he just doesn't *care* about me anymore!

BEN. You can't be sure of that.

ALICE. Oh, yes. Yes, I can. Today is our wedding anniversary. I was fixing something special for dinner. Pot roast. His favorite. He came home from work, looked in the pot, and said that's what he had for lunch.

BEN. And *was* it?

ALICE. Yes. Well, not the *same* pot roast, of course.

BEN. (*Exact same delivery: square-jawed ruggedness, slightly out front.*) I understand.

ALICE. Then—he just walked out.

BEN. Without a word?

ALICE. Oh, yes, he said a word.

BEN. What word?

ALICE. I can't say it.

BEN. (*Same bit.*) I understand.

ALICE. Do you? Really?

BEN. Yes. I do.

ALICE. You're very understanding.

BEN. Go on with your story.

ALICE. Well, I *cried,* of course.

BEN. Of course.

ALICE. Then I called *you.*

BEN. Why me?

ALICE. Why *not* you?

BEN. Because—well—under the circumstances—

ALICE. What circumstances?

BEN. Over these past few weeks, you've given me to understand that Don is very jealous. Yet here we are. Alone. You and I. And after all—

ALICE. (*Quoting, but since we can't hear quote-marks, it sounds pretty silly as she says sincerely:*) "I'm a man and you're a woman?"

BEN. (*After blank pause, murmurs uncertainly:*) Something like that.

ALICE. But Don is *gone.*

BEN. Are you quite sure?

ALICE. Oh, yes. When he walked out of the kitchen, I thought he'd come in here to sulk. I turned off the pot roast, then came right in here after him. Not a sign of him.

BEN. (*Same bit.*) I understand.

ALICE. I knew you would.

BEN. What are your plans?

ALICE. I suppose—first of all—I'll refrigerate the pot roast. Afterwards— Well, I simply can't think beyond that point. (*They sit silent a moment; then she says, brightly:*) Would you like a piece of fruit?

BEN. (*Looks at bowl, hesitates, then shakes his head.*) I'd better not.

ALICE. It's really quite good. . . .

BEN. I don't doubt it. But I'm on this diet.

ALICE. Surely one piece wouldn't hurt?

BEN. Perhaps not. But—a man's gotta do what a man's gotta do— (*Both abruptly stare out front, blinking in bewilderment.*) That's strange . . . ! Did you —ever have one of those things—?

ALICE. Where you think you've been somewhere before, done something before, said something before—?

BEN. Yes, one of those.

ALICE. Yes, I have.

BEN. Well, I just had one now.

ALICE. Strange, so did I.

BEN. Weird, isn't it!

ALICE. Yes. Almost—frightening. . . . But let's not think about that. Help me figure out what I should do! . . . Are you *sure* you won't have some of that fruit?

BEN. Much as I'd like to, no. Ordinarily, if I saw anything that delicious-looking, I'd swoop down on it like a bird of prey.

ALICE. Well, if you change your mind, feel free—to prey on my fruit— (*Both blink in bewilderment again, and very faintly we hear an oriental GONG; after a moment:*)

BEN. Odd. *What* did you just say—?

ALICE. *Prey* . . . on . . . my . . . *fruit* . . . (*The faint GONG sounds again; her fingertips go to temples*) This is insane. I must be losing my mind. I thought—I thought—

BEN. Steady. You're not going crazy. I heard it, too. Alice— (*Stands; she looks up at him.*) There is something very strange going on here, tonight . . .

ALICE. (*Fingers still at temples, stands slowly, on:*) And that's not all! Earlier—when I was fixing dinner—I nearly made a pot of *tea!*

BEN. (*As if it's a shocking admission.*) *Tea?!* (*As he realizes it isn't shocking, puzzledly.*) What's strange about *that?*

ALICE. I don't *like* tea. Neither does Don.

BEN. Then why—?

ALICE. That's just it! I don't know! It was about four o'clock, and a little voice in my head said, "Ah! Nearly tea-time!" And suddenly— (*Her fingertips go to the outer edges of her mouth.*) I found I had this terribly stiff upper lip—!

BEN. Luv-a-duck! (*Then he and she both react, wide-eyed, to his phrase.*) I say, that was a deucedly odd remark to make!

ALICE. So was that!

BEN. (*Looks Left and Right, as if the room menaced him.*) Do you know—I'm beginning to think this place is haunted—or worse—!

ALICE. Yes! Yes, I know what you mean! I've felt it, for hours and hours, now! Ever since eight o'clock!

BEN. But it's only just after eight, now—?!

ALICE. And that's another thing: It seems as though it will *never* be nine o'clock again! This hour—this particular hour—seems to just go on, and on, and on . . . !

BEN. (*Moves decisively toward phone.*) Then that does it! We need *professional* help!

ALICE. What? Who?

BEN. There's this woman—you may have heard of her—she has certain powers—or so they say, at any rate—in any case, what have we got to lose?

ALICE. You're going to call her?

BEN. *If* she's listed in the book . . . ! (*Flips telephone directory open, and instantly stabs index finger down on page.*) Yes, she is! (*Grabs up phone, speaks without dialing into mouthpiece.*) Hello, can you come right over, oh that's good of you, thank you! (*Hangs up and simultaneously DOORBELL rings.*) I thought she'd *never* get here! (*Springs to door, pulls it open, and* CAMILLE *enters, on:*)

CAMILLE. Sorry to be late. Got caught in traffic.

([*NOTE: from opening of phone book through* CAMILLE's *line should not take more than six seconds, total.*] CAMILLE, *by the way, is quite a sight: A bright bandanna is bound around her hair, Aunt-Jemima-fashion, she wears a large and colorful fringed shawl, gold-hoop earrings, many bracelets, carries a large woven-cord shopping bag, and has a pair of the blackest and bushiest V-slanted eyebrows in creation. She also speaks in the clipped singsong of a native of the West Indies, and she moves and talks with no-nonsense dispatch, in strong contrast to their hesitant attitudes.*)

BEN. Alice, I'd like you to meet—Mama Camille!

ALICE. The internationally famous voodoo priestess from the mysterious island of Haiti in the West Indies?!

BEN. Ah, you've heard of her?

ALICE. No. Just a lucky guess.

CAMILLE. (*Bustles directly to cocktail table, where she sets bag.*) There is much evil here. Me can feel it, deep in foot!

BEN. You mean "deep in *soul.*"

CAMILLE. (*As if saying, "Isn't that what I just said!":*) Deep in sole of *foot!* (*Drops to knees just above table, and as* ALICE *comes down to stand in front of Left armchair, and* BEN *in front of Right armchair, flanking her like votaries, she shuts her eyes, extends hands at arm's length and palms downward over table, sways left, right, back and forth, finally in a slow circular motion, moaning with each movement.*) Oh! . . . Oh! . . . Oh! . . . Oh! . . . Oh! . . .

BEN. Are you trying to call the spirits from beyond—?

CAMILLE. (*Stops movement but holds pose as she looks up at him.*) No. Trying to get comfortable on lumpy rug. (*Without waiting for comment, abruptly brings hands back toward face, rests backs of fingers on forehead, palms forward, shuts eyes.*) *Now* I will call upon spirits! Must have silence! Do not speak! (BEN *and* ALICE *wait apprehensively; after a moment,* CAMILLE *groans out words in a hollow voice.*) Spirits, can you hear me?! . . . Spirits, will you come to me?! . . . Spirits, where *are* you—? Where *are* you—? (*Then, as if they'd told her and surprised her.*) *Where—?!* (*Opens eyes, drops hands into lap, stands up.*)

BEN. Have you located the spirits?

CAMILLE. *Finally!* (*Heads right for bar, pours shot, tosses it off, gives high-pitched cackle of glee.*) Wheeeee! (*Comes back above table, but does not kneel this time.*) Now we ready to begin! First, we use juju-rattle, to seek out evil! (*Reaches into bag, brings out a maraca-like native rattle.*) You will follow me as I search. Stay behind at all times, so that Mama Camille remains between you and the evil. (*Starts to move Down Right, between* BEN *and table, but stops as* ALICE *lays hand upon her arm.*)

ALICE. Mama Camille—is there any *danger—?*

CAMILE. Yes. Great danger. Fearsome danger. Horrible danger. That is why— (*Abruptly hands rattle to* ALICE.) *you* better lead search.

ALICE. (*Exasperated.*) Mama Camille!

CAMILLE. Oh, all right! Stay very close! (*Takes rattle back, moves between* BEN *and table,* BEN *and* ALICE *follow after her, his hands on* CAMILLE's *waist,* ALICE's *hands on his, and all move in unison, five steps at a time, left-right-left-right-left-pause, with rattle shaking in tempo of their movement, thus: down-up-down-up-down-pause; they do this once, arriving near phonograph albums, and, on the pause:*) No. No evil here. (*Now they move, same tempo, up to bar, pause, and:*) No. No evil here. (*Same business Down to Right armchair.*) No . . . (*Same to Left armchair.*) No . . . (*From here on, pauses are quite short, because what trio is doing, without warning, on that five-counts-and-pause tempo, is, of course, "one-two-three-and-CON-*GA!", *with the word "No" coming on the last beat, and so, in similar manner, they move on to the telephone table: one-two-three-four-five—*) No! (*And over to window: one-two-three-four-five—*) No! (*And back over to cocktail table: one-two-three-four-five—*) No!

(*From this point, the trio-chain breaks up, and* ALICE *and* BEN *and* CAMILLE *each go their own direction, doing five-step and at the pause, with an enthusiastic hip-bump to left or right on the syllable by all, and* ALICE *and* BEN *joining on word:*)

ALICE, BEN, and CAMILLE. (*Five-step.*) No! (*Five-step.*) No! (*Five-step.*) No! (*Final five-step, during which* BEN *is laughing,* CAMILLE *cackling, and* ALICE *giggling, but at crucial point, in tempo,* ALICE *recovers sanity, and on final beat:*)

ALICE. *Whoa!* (CAMILLE *and* BEN *stop, shrug in embarrassment.*) This is getting us nowhere! Mama Camille—! (ALICE *is poised between window and phone,* BEN *near phonograph, and* CAMILLE*—facing Upstage toward* ALICE*—near taboret, on:*)

CAMILLE. (*Hands going imperiously over head as she cuts into* ALICE'S *line with shout:*) *Wait!* There is *thing* here! Strange thing! Horrible thing! (*As others freeze, frightened, she slowly lowers arms—then with a swift forward lunge, stomps to death some poor bug on the carpet before her, on:*) Gotcha!

ALICE. (*Exasperated.*) Oh, for heaven's sake—!

BEN. Mama Camille, *really,* now—!

CAMILLE. Sorry. Got carried away. (*Bustles up above*

table again, drops rattle into bag.) We try surefire thing, now! (*Rummages in bag as* ALICE *and* BEN *return to positions in front of respective armchairs; then:*) Ah, Now we get someplace! (*Triumphantly lifts rubber chicken out of bag, holds aloft.*) We sacrifice sacred rooster! Find out what evil spirits want!

BEN. It looks pretty dead right now!

CAMILLE. No, rooster still alive. Just had bad trip from Haiti.

ALICE. Mama Camille—tell me—why do chickens and roosters always figure so strongly in voodoo rituals?

CAMILLE. Many reason why! First—feathered bird is sacred to spirits!

BEN. Yes . . . ?

CAMILLE. Second—chicken is small enough for priestess to handle by herself!

ALICE. Yes . . . ?

CAMILLE. Finally—

BEN and ALICE. Yes . . . ?

CAMILLE. After voodoo ritual, chicken come in handy for *fricassee!* (*Rubs stomach reminiscently, on:*) A little rosé wine, a salad—

ALICE. (*Angry despair.*) Oh, this is ridiculous!

CAMILLE. (*Instantly grips her by arm.*) You no believe Mama Camille have mysterious powers?

ALICE. I—I'd *like* to believe it—but—can you *really* help me—?

CAMILLE. You name it, I do it.

ALICE. All right, then: Can you get my husband to *care?* Can you snap him out of his terrible apathy, and make him care—strongly—deeply—?!

CAMILLE. Well— I put on lots of perfume, fix hair, do nails—sit on his lap—chuck him under chin—

ALICE. Not for *you!* For *me!*

CAMILLE. Oh! That! Not sure. We see. You *trust* Mama Camille.

BEN. Oh, we do, we do!

CAMILLE. Okay. First, you give me five dollars.

ALICE. I'll pay you afterwards.

CAMILLE. How I know you will pay?

ALICE. Mama Camille must trust *me!*

CAMILLE. You drive hard bargain.

ALICE. Well, I'm *not* going to fork over five dollars for another *conga*-lesson!

CAMILLE. All right, all right! You both do everything me tell you, okay?

BEN. Whatever you say. Yes.

CAMILLE. Good! (*Sets chicken down on table, reaches into bag, takes out chain of colored magician-silks, proceeds to wrap them about extended wrists of* ALICE *and of* BEN, *linking them, on:*) First we must tie you with symbolic bonds, to show spirits you mean them no harm, or they will not approach!

ALICE. My, these are colorful! Does the color have any special meaning?

CAMILLE. Yes! Red is for blood, the color of heat, of anger! That is your husband!

BEN. How about the blue, what does that mean?

CAMILLE. Blue is for sorrow, for eyes that weep much tears, for unhappiness! That is wife!

ALICE. And how about the green?

CAMILLE. That is for Mama Camille's five dollars! Just a reminder!

ALICE. Oh, *really—!* Of all the stupid—!

CAMILLE. Silence! (ALICE *and* BEN *settle down, dubious but cooperative.*) That better. Now we get down to nitty-gritty! (*Rummages in bag, frowns, pats self searchingly at hips; then:*) Hey, either of you got a bucket on you?

BEN. Well, hardly! What do you want a *bucket* for?

CAMILLE. To catch blood when sacrifice rooster. Important to catch blood. Otherwise, terrible thing happen.

ALICE. What?

CAMILLE. You get permanent mess on carpet! (*Sights*

lamp.) Ah! There is just the thing Mama Camille need! (*Starts Downstage toward taboret.*)

ALICE. Mama Camille, it's bad enough letting you kill a chicken in the living room, but that's a priceless antique, and I really can't allow you to—!

CAMILLE. (*Picks up lamp, starts back toward table.*) Okay-okay, we just *pretend* to kill rooster. Spirits not know difference, anyhow. They *also* have bad trip from Haiti!

BEN. But look—if the spirits from Haiti are in a bad mood— Aren't you taking a big chance contacting them?

CAMILLE. (*Kneeling above table, setting lamp beside chicken.*) *Always* a little risky messing around with imported spirits! (*Starts to hold palms out over table, but stops at:*)

ALICE. (*Tugging silks from wrists, flinging them down.*) Well, *that* does it! Ben, this is the *stupidest* thing I *ever—!*

BEN. (*Reluctantly frees own wrists, drops rest of silks.*) Perhaps you're right, Alice. But things have been so strange, tonight, I was willing to try anything—!

CAMILLE. What things? Tell Mama Camille about strangeness!

ALICE. I wish I could. I really do. But it's all so—mixed up! I keep having this sense of terrible danger—for me—for Ben—for all of us! Even *you!*

BEN. Yes, and it has something to do with her husband, Don. We have these odd memories we can't quite grasp, can't quite account for—

CAMILLE. (*Puzzled, unconsciously rests hands upon lamp, during:*) Mama Camille not follow that. Me sure wish everything make sense—! (*Gapes as whistle of WIND roars up; lights dim, then come up full again as wind-noise fades;* CAMILLE *stands, wide-eyed.*) Holy Toledo! Hey, kids—all at once—I understand *everything!*

BEN. Mama Camille—what's happened to your accent?!

CAMILLE. Ben—Alice—don't you *know* me? I'm not from Haiti! I'm just plain Camille, your friend and neighbor! (*Holds up lamp, stares at it.*) This lamp! This holds the key to everything! Here—! (*Thrusts lamp into* ALICE's *hands.*) *You* try it!

ALICE. (*Blankly.*) I wish I understood what you're talking about—! (*WIND again, lights dim, come up, wind stops,* ALICE *gapes.*) Camille! Good grief! It's all so clear! So horribly clear! (*Instantly hands lamp to* BEN.) Quick, you too! There's no time to explain!

BEN. Explain what? What's going on? I wish you two would tell me—! (*WIND, lights, as before, and* ALICE *and* CAMILLE, *compelled by his wish on the lamp, now speak rapidly and mechanically, like a pair of parallel-programmed computer-robots.*)

CAMILLE and ALICE. The whole thing is *Don's* doing! He got hold of the lamp when he first showed up for the party! But at that time, Don was insanely jealous of Ben, jealous enough to want to kill him! But that revenge wasn't enough! He wanted to kill Ben—and then kill him again—and then again—and again and again! Over and over! Forever and ever! And that's what he happened to wish, in his mind, when he was holding the lamp! And he *got* his wish!

(*Robot-delivery stops; both women now move and speak normally—which in this circumstance means hysterically.*)

ALICE. Ben, don't you *remember* all of it? Don't you remember *any* of it?

BEN. I wish I *could—!* (*WIND, lights, etc.; then he gapes.*) Good grief, it's true! (*Looks at lamp in horror, lurches over to bar, sets it on top, steps back from it, wiping hands against thighs.*) It's horrible!

Fiendish! We've got to stop him! (*Whirls to face the women.*) How much time have we got—?!

ALICE. Only till nine o'clock!

CAMILLE. That's when we pop back to eight o'clock again, and start all over!

BEN. But will we remember all this? Will we know then what we know now?

ALICE. Probably not. That's why we've got to find Don—stop him—make him take back his dreadful wish—!

CAMILLE. (*Starts for door.*) Come on, then! He can't be *too* far! He's got to get back here before nine, to take a potshot at Ben or Alice or the *two* of you! (*Pulls open door.*)

ALICE. Wait! He might be out there in the hall, waiting—! (CAMILLE *closes door.*)

BEN. But he won't shoot! Don't you see? He's doing this as his revenge on *you!* So he won't do anything to us unless you're there to watch and suffer while he does it!

ALICE. But—I want to come *with* you—! Don't leave me here alone!

CAMILLE. No, Ben's right! (*Opens door.*) We'll go try and find Don! You lock this door and don't let *anybody* in till we get back, you hear me?!

ALICE. I—all right! But please hurry!

BEN. We'll do our best! Keep your fingers crossed!

(BEN *and* CAMILLE *exit;* ALICE *frantically shuts door, fumbles for lock, finds it, locks it—and as she is doing so,* DON—*the revolver in his hand—steps quietly out of wardrobe behind her, shuts door, waits there; then* ALICE *turns wearily, sees him, reacts with terror.*)

ALICE. (*Screams the name.*) *Don—!*

DON. (*Cackling.*) Yes! Yes, your husband has been here *all* along, heard *everything*. . . . (*Advances toward her, aiming gun.*)

ALICE. (*Backing from him, toward Downstage Left.*) Don—listen to reason—you've got to understand—there was never anything between me and Ben—you've got to believe that—!

DON. (*Relentlessly moving down after her, step by step.*) I'd *like* to. I know you won't believe me, but I'd *like* to believe that. But I ask you—how can I? Your story—the magic lessons—did you ever hear anything so stupid?

ALICE. (*Near window, now.*) But Don, the truth *always* sounds stupid! Don't you think, if I *had* been deceiving you, that I could have made up a better lie than *that?!*

DON. Of course you could have. But maybe you thought that I was stupid enough to believe you.

ALICE. Oh, Don . . . Don . . . ! (*Abruptly turns, rushes to window, screams.*) Help! Help, somebody! *Please!* (*Sees* DON *rushing upon her, leaps away from window, backs downward to area near taboret, drops to knees facing him.*) Don, you've *got* to listen—*got* to believe—Don, I *swear—!*

DON. (*Reaches out with left hand, takes her gently by throat, holds revolver forward for her inspection.*) Do you see this? There are just two bullets left in it! One of them is for me—the other is for you!

ALICE. (*Hopefully:*) *In that order—?!*

DON. (*Irritated.*) Of course not! What do you take me for?!

ALICE. (*Gets angrily to her feet.*) The man I love. Or thought I loved. But—you see—when you began to act this way—I realized —you weren't the man I had first loved— (*DOORBELL and loud KNOCKING begin.*)

BEN. (*Off.*) Alice! Alice, are you all right?!

DON. (*Clamps hand over* ALICE's *mouth, turns head slightly Upstage, trills in falsetto tone.*) Yes, Ben, darling! Everything's just fine and dandy!

CAMILLE. (*Off.*) Alice, what's the matter with your voice?!

DON. (*Desperate, whispers to* ALICE.) You answer her! And don't make any mistakes! (*Unclamps hand from her mouth, holds gun to her head.*)

ALICE. (*Quavering with fear, trying to conceal it.*) It's all right, Camille! I'm fine! Now you and Ben go away!

BEN. (*Off.*) Go *away!?* Alice, it's five minutes till nine o'clock!

ALICE. Oh, *no! Don,* for the love of heaven—!

CAMILLE. (*Off.*) Ben! He's *in* there with her! Break the door down! (*Sound of SHOULDER-STRIKE against door.*)

BEN. (*Off.*) Ow!

CAMILLE. (*Off.*) Harder, hit it harder!

BEN. (*Off.*) That's as hard as I can hit! I nearly busted my shoulder!

DON. (*Turns, the better to shout.*) Keep back, both of you, I'm warning you! (ALICE, *seeing her chance, springs for his gun-hand, grabs wrist with both hands and hangs on.*) Hey! Let go of me!

ALICE. (*Shrieking as they wrestle back and forth.*) Ben! Camille! Hurry!

BEN. (*Off.*) Coming, Alice! (*SHOULDER-STRIKE.*) Ow!

ALICE. Please! It's almost nine o'clock!

CAMILLE. (*Off.*) Get out of the way and let *me* try!

DON. Alice, let go of my arm—! (*With a CRASH, door flies open,* CAMILLE *appearing at full run, shoulder forward, which carries her right off again down corridor;* BEN *pokes his head around corner, and* DON *manages to twist his arm that way and FIRE gun;* BEN *pops out again, instantly.*) Damn it, will you let go—?!

ALICE. He's only got one bullet left! Help me! Help me!

DON. (*Pulls free of her with a wrench, but revolver

drops to floor, as she sprawls face-down near it, and he staggers, off-balance, back toward bar.) Hey! Alice, darling, listen to me—! (BEN *and* CAMILLE *appear from respective areas, now, and each manages to grab* DON *by one arm, dragging him struggling backward till they are all up against bar, as* ALICE, *grabbing up revolver, gets to her feet and holds it trained on him.*) Alice, wait! You wouldn't shoot me, your own husband— (*Pulls free, grabs lamp.*) over this silly little *lamp?!*

ALICE. Why not?! How many times tonight have you shot *me?!*

DON. I wish I knew! (*WIND; then:*) Hey, I *did* shoot you! But it was an accident!

CAMILLE. *What?*

DON. It's true! (*Replaces lamp on bar.*) Every time Alice got shot, it was an accident! When I was shooting off the lock— When I tripped on my way toward her— When *Camille* shot her— *Once* she even shot *herself!* I *never* intended that *Alice* should be hurt—! Just *Ben!* (BEN *reacts with huffy glare.*)

ALICE. (*Revolver wavering.*) But Don— I've *got* to! I *must* shoot you! You're the one *behind* this whole thing, and it's nearly nine o'clock! (*All freeze as Westminster-CHIME melody begins playing.*)

BEN. (*Breaks paralyzed mood with:*) It's going to strike nine! Shoot, Alice, shoot!

DON. No, wait! It won't do any good! I've *already* been shot, and it didn't change a thing!

CAMILLE. Alice, he's right! I remember! When he dropped the gun and it went off!

ALICE. But what can I do?! W can't just *stand* here—?! (*Melody has finished; clock is now STRIKING hour of nine: ONE . . .*)

BEN. You'd better do *something!* (*TWO . . .*) I don't want to spend the rest of my life getting bumped off! (*THREE . . .*)

DON. (*Drops to knees.*) I won't do it any more! I

promise! I was crazed with jealousy! (*FOUR . . .*)

CAMILLE. But Don, if we go back to eight o'clock again, you won't *remember* what you promised! (*FIVE . . .*)

ALICE. Oh, no! She's right! (*SIX . . .*)

BEN. Wait! I've got it! I know what to do! (*SEVEN . . .*)

CAMILLE. *What?!*

DON. Say something, *quick!* (*EIGHT . . .*)

BEN. *The lamp!* Destroy the *lamp!*

ALICE. It's *behind* you! *Hit the dirt!*

(*And as* DON, CAMILLE *and* BEN *all dive forward flat onto floor, and the final stroke of NINE sounds, and the lamp on the bar is exposed to* ALICE'S *view and she FIRES at it, and the lamp FLIES into the air and falls behind bar—there is a rush of WIND, and total BLACKOUT, and we hear:*)

DON. Alice!

ALICE. Don, where are you?!

CAMILLE. Who handed me this *chicken?!*

BEN. Was that *you—?!*

(*Over next four speeches, there is an insane background MONTAGE-SOUND of all the clock-strike noises: hen-clucks, cuckoos, police whistles, churchbells, regular chimes, etc.*)

CAMILLE. (*Giggling.*) Ben! Stop that! Shame on you!

DON. Sorry, Camille! I thought you were Alice!

BEN. Then who am *I* holding?!

ALICE. Ben! Let go of me! (*Then WIND-noise starts up, louder and louder, on:*)

DON. What's that dirty rat doing to my wife *now—?!* (*WIND-roar drowns out all other sound; holds for about three seconds; then fades, wheezes, and stops.*)

(*Lights come up; Stage is empty; then* CAMILLE *enters from corridor to kitchen, looking as at top of show; her manner is stunned, frantic; she looks about, confused, fingers going into her hair at temples; she looks on bar; then she comes Down and looks on taboret; DOORBELL; she rushes to door and opens it.*)

CAMILLE. Don! Alice! (*They enter, frantically, arm-in-arm both from affection and fear.*)

DON. Camille! Are you okay?!

ALICE. We suddenly found ourselves in the hall outside your door! I've never been so scared in my life!

CAMILLE. (*With hysteria-born logic.*) It *is* a pretty creepy hall!

DON. Oh, damn! Don't you *remember*— I mean— I *know* this will sound *insane* if you *don't,* but—

CAMILLE. Of course I remember. I suddenly found myself in the kitchen, making hors d'oeuvres!

ALICE. (*Anxiously.*) But you're okay—? No oriental or British inclinations—?

CAMILLE. I—I guess not. It's all so terrifying.

DON. (*Brightening, getting calmer.*) Wait—if you're okay—and we're okay—and you were making hors d'oeuvres— it must be the *party* again!

ALICE. (*Delighted, relieved.*) Only *now* we're *all right!*

CAMILLE. And the *lamp* is gone—I had it with me in the *kitchen,* the *first* time around. *Now* I can't find it *anywhere!*

DON. And good riddance to it! (*DOORBELL.*) Hey, that must be Ben! Boy, do *I* ever owe *him* an apology!

ALICE. *I'll* get the door . . . (*Goes to it, takes knob, holds for:*)

CAMILLE. Wow, am I ever relieved! We should spend this whole party counting our blessings!

ALICE. You can say *that* again! (*Opens door, stares out, gasps and backs away on:*) *Ben!*

BEN. (*Enters, dressed as "Ben-Boy," carrying chicken.*) Hi, neighbor-lady! I brought your chicken!

OTHERS. (*A shriek of horror, all but idiotically grinning* BEN *going into ghastly shock.*) Oh, *noooo-oooo!*

(*WIND-sound comes up, mingled with hollow diabolical laughter, as lights fade, and:*)

THE CURTAIN FALLS

CURTAIN CALL

Lamp is back on taboret [if this is not practical, then it should be in DON'S *pocket], and Stage is empty, as curtain opens [Or lights come up, depending on how this is staged]. Then* BEN*—still as "Ben-Boy," of course—enters through door, comes Down Left of chairs to Center Stage and takes solo bow, then gestures flamboyantly up toward corridor-to-kitchen entrance.* CAMILLE *enters from there, comes Down Right of chairs to take Center-Stage solo bow, and remains on* BEN'S *Right as both of them gesture flamboyantly up toward door.* ALICE *enters there, comes Down Left of chairs to* BEN'S *side, takes solo bow. Then all three gesture flamboyantly up toward corridor, except that* DON *pops out of cabinet, instead, and comes Down to* ALICE'S *Left almost before others notice him, and takes solo bow. [*] Then all join hands and take unified company-bow. Then* DON *moves Down Left, and* CAMILLE *Down Right, and they take unified bow.* BEN *and* ALICE *almost join them, but* *suddenly become aware that they are still holding hands. They look at hands, then into each other's eyes—and then they go into terrific kiss-clinch.* DON *turns, sees them, reacts, then takes lamp, crouches with fiendish grin on his face, and furiously starts rubbing lamp.* CAMILLE *sees this, and covers her face, shaking her head, as* ALICE *and* BEN *keep kissing,* DON *keeps rubbing fiendishly, and—*

THE CURTAIN FALLS

* At this point, if you wish, all four performers can make a flamboyant gesture up toward either the corridor or the cabinet (if it has a false back, for easier costume-changes and appearances), and a hand can come out holding the rubber chicken by the neck, and the foursome can lead the applause for it. Then it is pulled back in, and they go on to their company-bow, and so forth, as indicated above.

RECOMMENDATIONS

1. Use a *hollow* rubber chicken. The solid foam rubber chickens do not fold up small enough to be stashed undetectably in pockets, etc.

2. Use a 6-shot cap pistol for the revolver. The 6-shot pistols have a rotating six-dot disc that fires every time, without the chance of a miss-firing that can happen with strip-caps; and a gun that fires blanks is too dangerous for close-up use.

3. The ropes on Ben in Act Two, Scene Three, are put on him thus: Hold an 18-inch length of heavy cord in a U-shape so that it is across the front of his ankles with the ends going to the back alongside his feet; bring the ends forward between his feet *under* the piece across the front, then back *over* this piece and between his ankles to the back again. This can be kept in place by Ben simply holding his ankles together, but can fall off as soon as he spreads his feet apart. Wrists are bound similarly.

4. Since moving about in the darkness of a blackout is dangerous enough just for the foursome in the cast, it might be well if the cast members themselves dealt with the clearing of, and presetting of, various items as each scene ends *during* an act. Between entire acts, of course, the stage crew can handle the placement or removal of the props.

5. The revolver should be completely loaded before each scene, even if there seem to be enough caps left for the upcoming scene. It's better to waste a few caps each evening than to be caught short onstage at a crucial moment with a silent gun.

6. During each act, each scene can end with darkness immediately following actual performer's final remark of surprise to lamp, so that the WIND and HOLLOW DISEMBODIED VOICE can bridge gap

as next scene is set up, melding right into WEST-MINSTER-CHIME effect, still in darkness, which opens subsequent scene, so that each act plays as a unity, despite scene-multiplicity.

7. To help refresh audience's memory as each new act begins, it might be wise, after curtain opens but before chimes begin, to have last-speaking performer repeat the "wish" line in darkness, and the "voice" to repeat its sinister interpretation of that wish.* (An alternative to this is to actually *skip* the "voice" at the end of the act, ending instead on the performer's line of surprise, with WIND then coming up in darkness at curtain, and then—as just suggested—have the performer repeat the line in darkness at start of act, the "voice" say its follow-up line,* and then blend into chimes which begin act.)

8. In the premiere performance of this show, the director opted to make Act Two Scene One the Fourth Scene of Act One, and then begin Act Two with the Nagasaki sequence. It played just splendidly, so this restructuring is a feasible alternative. It all depends upon how long you wish each act to run, the problems of setting up for the next scene, costume changes, and the like. As long as the eight scenes remain in the same order, the show plays logically and well. But if you do move a scene back, be sure to observe the scene-melding and act-starting suggestions in recommendations 6 and 7, above.

THE AUTHOR

* When "voice" *begins* Nagasaki scene, omit train whistle. Also, if "Ben-Boy" scene begins Act Two (as here written) rather than ending Act One, omit "Okay, Ben, if that's the way you want it" from VOICE at start of Act Two, but use preceding phrases by VOICE, of course, up to that line.

PROPERTY LIST

ACT ONE

Scene 1:

Preset—liquor and glasses on bar

Carried on by—

DON:

revolver and chicken in topcoat pockets

CAMILLE:

ice bucket, tissue-wrapped lamp

BEN:

colored silks in breast pocket

Scene 2:

Cleared—

used glasses, lamp

Carried on by—

DON:

revolver and silks in jacket

CAMILLE:

ice bucket, tissue-wrapped lamp

BEN:

chicken inside jacket, tray of hors d'oeuvres

Scene 3:

Cleared—

used glasses, colored silks, Don's hat and coat from wardrobe

Preset—

lamp on taboret, chicken on table

Carried on by—

CAMILLE:

dressbox

DON:

revolver in hand

ACT TWO

Scene 1:

Cleared—

silks from table

Preset—

lamp on taboret, chicken back of bar, newspaper comics for Don and knitting gear for Camille

Scene 2:

Cleared—

newspaper comics, knitting

Preset—

lamp on taboret on table, flute for Alice

Scene 3:

Cleared—

taboret, flute

Preset—

lamp on bar, violin-case containing pair of pliers and chicken behind bar

Carried on by—

CAMILLE:

revolver

Scene 4:

Cleared—

violin-case, chicken

Preset—

lamp on taboret, goblets in foursome's hands, revolver in Don's inner pocket

ACT THREE

Cleared—

goblets

Preset—

bowl of fruit on table, lamp on taboret, kerchief for Alice, Don himself inside wardrobe with gun

Carried on by—

CAMILLE:

bag containing chicken, juju rattle, silks

SOUND EFFECTS (*needed in various combinations and repetitions*)

Doorbell. Telephone bell. Westminster chimes (16-note melody which precedes striking of hour). Chimes, cuckoos, gongs, police whistles, churchbells, hen-clucks—all to strike the hour. Dance music from radio. Loud knocking at door. Shoulder-strikes on door. Gunshots (those not performed in view of audience, such as when gun falls to floor and fires, Offstage shots, etc.). Very faint gong for Act Three. Montage of chimes, clucks, gongs, whistles, etc. for Act Three. Wind-noises for lamp-effect alone. Wind-noises plus pre-taped speeches and demonic laughter for ends of scenes. Train-whistle for end of "Nagasaki" lines by VOICE.

STAGE SETTING
FOR
"WHO'S ON FIRST?"

[For thrust-stage, simply eliminate left and right walls and hang window-frame on wires]

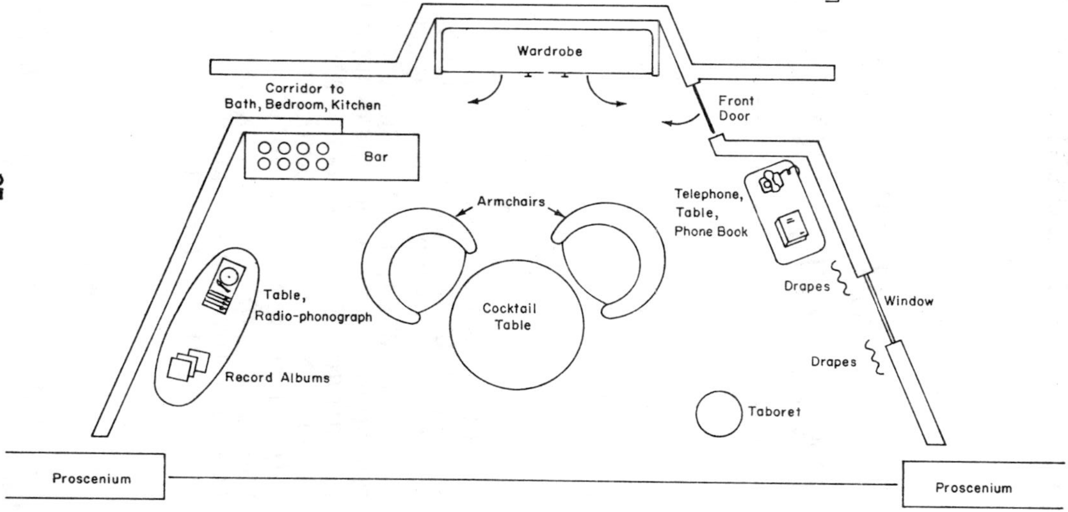

Wardrobe
Corridor to
Bath, Bedroom, Kitchen
Front
Door
Bar
Armchairs
Telephone,
Table,
Phone Book
Table,
Radio-phonograph
Cocktail
Table
Drapes
Window
Drapes
Record Albums
Taboret
Proscenium
Proscenium